The Promised Land

Also by Isabelle Holland:

The Journey Home

Behind the Lines

The Promised Land

Isabelle Holland

**SCHOLASTIC
HARDCOVER**

Scholastic Inc.
New York

Library of Congress Cataloging-in-Publication Data
Holland, Isabelle.
The Promised Land / Isabelle Holland.
p. cm.
Summary: Orphaned by their mother's death, two Irish Catholic
sisters find a home with a kind Protestant couple on the Kansas
frontier, but their new life is suddenly threatened by the
appearance of their uncle, who is determined to take them back to
New York and their "true" religion.
ISBN 0-590-47176-7
[1. Orphans—Fiction. 2. Sisters—Fiction. 3. Prejudices—
Fiction. 4. Foster home care—Fiction. 5. Frontier and pioneer
life—Kansas—Fiction. 6. Kansas—Fiction.] I. Title.
PZ7.H7083Pr 1996
[Fic]—dc20   94-42284
CIP
AC

12 11 10 9 8 7 6 5 4 3 2 1   6 7 8 9/9 0 1/0

Printed in the U.S.A.   37

First printing, April 1996

One

Maggie woke up early, as she always did. The corner of the main room of the Russells' house was still dark. Sitting up in bed, she could see through the window that the sun was just showing over the horizon in the east, throwing a path of light across the dark fields. During her three years in Kansas Maggie had watched the sun come up almost every morning, and it still thrilled and delighted her, as did the sight of fields covered with new green shoots and the huge endless sky.

How wonderful it all was, she thought, the endless prairie, stretching to the remote horizon, seemingly flat but, with its shadowed dips and hollows, not flat at all. And clean and fresh and sweet-smelling.

Beside her, ten-year-old Annie slept soundly,

her fair hair spread in waves over her pillow.

"Annie," Maggie said, gently nudging her sister, "wake up!"

When Annie didn't move, Maggie nudged her again. "Annie, it's time to get up."

When Annie still didn't move, Maggie drew up her knees and put her arms around them. "Isn't Bessie waiting?"

Annie's eyelids flickered. Then she turned onto her back. Her blue eyes opened wide. Maggie looked down at her and grinned. Annie had as hard a time getting up as she did going to bed. Maggie was the opposite.

Suddenly Annie sat up. "Lilac!"

"What about Lilac?" Maggie asked, swinging her legs onto the floor. "She can't be expecting again. Her kittens are barely six weeks old."

Annie was already out of bed and pulling on her stockings. "No. It's just that one doesn't seem to be getting milk and I want to get some from Bessie before Uncle James milks her."

Maggie smiled. "You and your animals!"

At that moment Aunt Priscilla came out of the main bedroom.

"Good morning, Maggie, good morning, Annie," she said cheerfully. She stopped and looked out the cabin window. "It's going to be a beautiful day."

Maggie, who had poured water from the bucket under the sink into a bowl on the table, was washing her face. As she reached for the towel, she glanced out the window again. "It will indeed."

The sun was now fully up, lighting the fields and the barn. Uncle James, the first up, was already drawing water from the well.

Annie, now dressed, ran out the door to the barn.

"Breakfast will be in a few minutes!" Aunt Priscilla called after her. "Tell Uncle James."

Maggie, tying her apron on, smiled as Aunt Priscilla brought eggs and bacon from the outside locker. "What would you like me to do first?"

"I'd like you to slice the bread and put on the hot water. Then please help Mama get ready for her breakfast. I'll have her tray —"

She was interrupted by a loud wail rising from a crib in the Russells' bedroom.

"Goodness!" Aunt Priscilla said. "I thought William would sleep a few more minutes. He's probably hungry. Maggie, do you think you could see to him? I'll get Mama's tray ready."

Maggie put down the knife with which she had been slicing the bread and went into the small, neat bedroom.

Beside the big bed was a cradle that Uncle James had built when he and his wife learned that they were finally going to become parents. One of the reasons they'd agreed to take in a

3

child from the orphan train was because of their failure, after many years of marriage, to have any children of their own. Two years after Maggie and Annie had come to live with them, William, now one, had arrived.

"All right, William," Maggie said, bending over the cradle and picking up the baby. She felt his diaper as she walked back into the main room. "You need changing." She put him down on the bed she and Annie shared in the cabin's main room. "And I know you're hungry."

"So is this kitten," Annie said, coming back in from the barn, followed by a large white dog with a brindled spot on its side. "Hungry, I mean." With one hand she was cradling a tiny black kitten wrapped in a towel. With the other she was carrying a bucket containing a little milk. "I was right," she said, putting down the bucket and placing the kitten gently on the table. "Lilac doesn't have enough milk for all the kittens. This one isn't getting any and will starve. I brought some of Bessie's milk to heat." She was pouring milk into a small pan when Uncle James came in.

His eyes fell on Spot stretched out on the floor near Annie. "You know I don't like animals in the cabin," he said. "And is that a *kitten* on the table?"

"Yes. She's not getting any of Lilac's milk.

She's smaller than the others and they push her away."

"Annie —" Uncle James started.

"I know you think that if an animal can't fend for itself it should be allowed to die, but I think it's a shame! If we just give it some milk it might grow bigger than any of the others." She took a breath. "AND be a better mouser," she added.

"And it might not. Annie, we don't need any more cats anyway. Lilac and one of her kittens is enough. So let's keep one of the healthier ones." Uncle James reached his hand toward the tiny creature bundled in a towel on the table.

But Annie snatched it up. "I've promised some of the children in school the other kittens," she said. "So there's no need to drown any. And this'll be a good mouser, I promise!"

She stood there, her pretty face set, her corn-colored hair falling on her shoulders, the kitten held in her hand against her chest. Then her mouth broke into a radiant smile that seemed to light up her eyes. "*Please*, Uncle James!"

Maggie, busy trying to get a fresh diaper on the lively and wiggling William, watched with interest, amusement, and a touch of wistfulness. Once she would have described Uncle James's face as severe — a severity emphasized by his neatly trimmed beard. He was re-garded in the church and among his fellow farmers and townspeople as a strong man, a stout upholder of what he thought to be right, which included an unsentimental approach to farm animals. But he was no match for Annie, who loved and cared for anything with four legs.

"We have no time to coddle animals," Uncle James went on. "And we don't have any milk to waste either —" he started, then stopped. After a minute he walked to the door and turned. "I'm going out for more firewood. How soon is breakfast going to be ready?"

"Any minute now," Aunt Priscilla said, put-ting a cup of coffee, a plate with one egg and one strip of bacon, and some sliced and but-tered bread onto a tray. "Maggie, when you've finished changing William, would you keep an eye on his oatmeal and milk in the pan there, and make sure it doesn't get too hot? Annie, would you set the table?"

Annie was putting a towel end soaked with warm milk into the kitten's mouth. "I'll do it as soon as I've finished —"

"No, Annie," Aunt Priscilla said gently. "Now."

Annie sighed and removed the milk-soaked corner of the towel from the kitten's mouth.

She carried the kitten, still snuggled in the rest of the towel, over to the bed, then put it in the middle of the quilt a few feet from where Maggie was finishing pinning the fresh diaper on William. Then she quickly set the table.

Maggie glanced at the tiny kitten and smiled a little. "What about Spot?" she asked and nodded toward the big dog on the floor beside the stove, his nose down on his paws, his eyes on the bed.

"He likes the kitten," Annie said. "He won't hurt it."

At that minute William, who had pulled himself to his feet, started jumping up and down on the bed. "Ma! Maggie!" he yelled.

Maggie went over, picked him up, kissed his cheek, then put him down on the floor. "Now be good," she said, "and don't get under our feet. And don't scare the kitten!"

She glanced at Annie. "Keep an eye on William, will you?" She went over to the stove, tested the oatmeal with her finger, and removed it from the heat. Then she broke eggs into the big pan where more bacon was sizzling.

As Aunt Priscilla emerged from her mother's room, Uncle James came in carrying some firewood, which he put down behind the stove.

"Breakfast, everybody," Aunt Priscilla said.

She picked up William and sat down at the table with him on her lap. Everyone sat down and Uncle James said the blessing.

As the others ate, Aunt Priscilla began feeding William his oatmeal. "My goodness, you were hungry!"

In a few minutes Maggie pushed away her empty plate and got up. "Aunt Priscilla, let me do that for you. You're not getting any breakfast." She carried William back to her place, sat down, and pulled the oatmeal over toward her. "Now, little brother," she said with playful sternness, "let's see if you can finish this."

"You know, Aunt Priscilla," Annie said, eyeing William from across the table. "Sometimes I think he looks like you, and sometimes I think he's like Uncle James."

"He definitely has Uncle James's chin," Maggie said, easing the spoon into William's mouth. "But he has your blue eyes, Aunt Priscilla."

"I bet he'll have a beard like Uncle James," Annie said.

"Annie!" Maggie protested. "Give him — and us — a little time in between."

"Tempus fugit," Uncle James said, with a slight smile. "I'm going to have to go into town later," he added. "We need more feed." He glanced at his wife. "Do you want anything?"

"I need some cotton goods for Maggie's and Annie's spring dresses. They've just about grown out of last year's."

Maggie glanced at her with affection. "I can still get into my blue one," she said. "Although it's a bit of a squeeze."

"Yes, but you really ought to have a new one for the spring lunch and fair at church. I noticed the last time you wore it, it was tight here and there. And Annie's is much too small. I guess I'll go with you, James. And we mustn't forget to go to the post office."

Uncle James smiled. "Are you expecting mail from your Southern kin?"

"I think Mama might be. She asked this morning if you were going to check the mail."

Annie took her eyes off the kitten long enough to say, "Do they still hate the North, Aunt Priscilla?"

"Hate's a strong word, Annie. And it's wrong to hate," Aunt Priscilla replied.

"Anyway," Uncle James said, "we're all one nation again." He glanced at his wife. "Do you think Mama might agree to that, Priscilla?"

"Oh yes. Even though she's very loyal to the South, I think in her heart of hearts she thought the war might have been avoided."

"But slavery's wrong, Aunt Priscilla!" Annie said.

"Yes. There's no question about that."

Maggie looked over at Uncle James, who was busy wiping up the last of his eggs with a piece of bread. He had served all four years of the war in the Union Army, first under General McClellan and then under General Meade. He and Aunt Priscilla had met and fallen in love in Washington, where her very Southern family lived and where they were married in the face of her family's heated opposition.

As she put William on the floor in front of her and started playing with him, Maggie thought about the days before she and Annie had come out to Kansas on the orphan train. When her Irish immigrant parents were still alive, they all lived in Five Points, the terrible New York City slum where pigs and starving dogs rooted in foul, fetid streets, where three and four families were crowded into a single room, where so many of the newly arrived Irish died of tuberculosis, as had her mother.

Her eyes went to the window of the little house Uncle James had built himself, to the light green fields that covered the hills outside and the shiny dark green of Aunt Priscilla's vegetable garden and the golden hay stacked outside the barn. More than anything else the view through that window represented the difference between how terrible life had been for her and for Annie — despite their dying

10

mother's best efforts — and what it was now.

One moment in that other life had burned itself into her memory: She was eleven and it was the day before Christmas. She and some other children were trying to sell matches outside A. P. Stewart, the big New York department store on Broadway and Tenth Street. She had run over to a carriage that had stopped and held matches up to a lady stepping down to go into the store. The lady was beautifully dressed and a faint scent of lavender preceded her. When Maggie ran up, the lady's face turned away as though Maggie and the other ragged children offended her. But with one gloved hand she'd pressed a dime into Maggie's . . .

"What are you thinking about, Maggie?" Aunt Priscilla asked.

"About that lady in the carriage outside A. P. Stewart's. The one I told you about. And how she looked at us."

"You don't have to think about that now," Uncle James said.

Aunt Priscilla got up to take up the plates. "You know how James and I love you. We couldn't love you more if you were our own. You belong here."

"I know, Aunt Priscilla. We both do. Don't we, Annie?"

Annie reached up and hugged Aunt Priscilla.

11

"Absolutely!" And then she hugged Uncle James, who was sitting beside her.

Maggie watched a little enviously. She could never do that.

"Go on now!" Uncle James said sternly. But, unexpectedly, he leaned over and gave Annie a hug. "Now," he said, as though to make up for this display of feeling, "you're going to have to hurry to get to school. And I still think it's a waste of time to try and save that kitten!" Then he walked out of the cabin so Annie couldn't answer.

"You know, Annie dear, he's not as hard as he sounds — or thinks he ought to be, don't you?" Aunt Priscilla said.

"Yes. He really loves me. But he's wrong about Blackie."

"So you've named the kitten," Maggie said, amused.

"Yes. You can't drown somebody you know!"

"Annie!" Aunt Priscilla said. "That's a . . . a . . ." She looked both amused and shocked.

"But it's true, isn't it?" Annie asked.

Aunt Priscilla sighed. She picked up William who was trying to climb back onto the bed. "When you put it like that it certainly sounds it." She eyed the kitten sleeping on the quilt. "That kitten's hardly the size of a large mouse. I wonder if it really can survive."

"Of course it can, Aunt Priscilla."

The frail-looking woman glanced at Annie. "Yes, I heard what you told James. Did you really promise the other kittens to the children at school? Or did you just make it up on the spur of the moment?"

Annie's blue eyes opened wide. "I —" Then she giggled. "Well, I knew I could. Remember? I got the last batch adopted."

"Yes, I know. But you have to realize that most people have barn cats of their own, Annie. They don't need ours."

"I don't want Uncle James to drown them."

"Would you rather just let them wander out and starve or freeze to death in the winter? You know Lilac will lead them away when they're old enough to take care of themselves. Mother cats do that."

Annie didn't reply, but a stubborn look came across her face.

"Maggie," Aunt Priscilla said. "You're going to have to leave for school soon, but could you get Mama's tray and help her to sit up and dress? I want to fix your lunch and get ready to leave with James."

Mrs. Vanderpool's imperious voice sounded from her bedroom. "Yes, Maggie, I've been waiting."

Mrs. Vanderpool occupied one of the cabin's

two bedrooms. As Maggie walked in she barked, "What's going on out there? Whatever is James scolding about now?"

While the old lady might have difficulty moving, her mind and her curiosity were as sharp as ever, so Maggie told her about the debate over the kitten.

Mrs. Vanderpool grunted. A woman in her seventies with bad arthritis, she stood shakily as Maggie helped her into her dress. "Well," she said when her dress was buttoned up. "My money is on Annie. One way or another she'll get her way. You watch! James can never say no to her."

"You're right," Maggie said tersely.

The old lady glanced at her shrewdly. Then, as Maggie knelt down to help her with her shoes, she asked, "How's school?"

"Fine. We're reading *David Copperfield*."

"How do you like it?"

"It's wonderful!" Maggie said enthusiastically, looping up the last shoelace. "I'll never forget when his mother dies!" She looked up and smiled at the older woman. "There's a character in the book who reminds me of you."

"Indeed?" Mrs. Vanderpool's brows went up. "And who would that be?"

"Betsey Trotwood."

Mrs. Vanderpool made a face. "Because we're both old? Hardly flattering, but . . ." she

14

paused and smiled, "not far from the mark." She glanced at Maggie. "I bet not everybody in class feels the way you do about *David Copperfield.*"

Maggie laughed. "Tom likes it," she said, and blushed.

"Maybe he does or maybe he likes it because of you."

Maggie blushed again as she stood up. "No, Mrs. Vanderpool. He really likes it."

"And what does that spiteful, pretty little thing, Ellen somebody, think of that? Now help me out to my chair."

Maggie reached out her hands, which were grasped by Mrs. Vanderpool. "Not much. She makes sarcastic remarks all the time. You'd think she'd know the other girls — at least some of them — and Tom think she's mean."

"Good for him. The boy isn't stupid. Now hand me my cane."

Maggie helped the old lady across the bedroom and into the main room. "The only person who really tries to fight her is Annie. I tell her not to do it, but she goes ahead anyway."

"Annie will always follow her heart and her impulse — bless her. She loves you, though you're so different, and she loves her animals. And she loves her fantasies."

Maggie stopped and smiled. "She does that." For the first time in a while she heard the touch of Irish in her own voice. "I didn't know anyone else noticed."

"Well, it's pretty obvious — at least to me. When Annie isn't thinking about what she's doing, which is a large part of the time, she's imagining things so clearly she's there doing them. Why are you staring at me? Don't you know it yourself?"

After a minute Maggie said, "Sister Catherine at St. Andrew's in New York said Annie had a head full of pictures."

"What a wonderful way of putting it! That describes it exactly."

Maggie laughed.

"Did I hear Priscilla say they're going into town?"

"Yes. Uncle James has to get some feed, and Aunt Priscilla wants to buy some material to make dresses for Annie and me." Maggie paused and then said, "She's wonderful to us — just like we were her own." She hesitated, then said, "Like Ma did when we were little — as much as she could, given the bad harvests, terrible conditions, and no money. And in New York she was too ill."

As so often happened when she talked about her mother, Maggie felt the beginning of tears. She shook her head to get rid of the feeling.

"Anything the matter?" Mrs. Vanderpool asked gently.

"No." Emotion always frightened Maggie. Then she smiled. "No," she said, and looked at the old lady who was sitting in her chair, her eyes fixed tenderly on Maggie. Quickly Maggie picked up a book and glanced at the title. "*Middlemarch*," she said. "What a funny title. What does it mean?"

"It's the name of a town."

"Do you like it?"

"Very much indeed. It's only just been published. A friend in England sent it to me. George Eliot is a wonderful writer." Mrs. Vanderpool gazed at the fifteen-year-old girl who was so near young womanhood. "I think you'd like it. It's about Dorothea, a very earnest and responsible young woman who is serious about life. Who loves books." She smiled a little. "Her sister wasn't like her, either."

Maggie turned the book over in her hands. "Did he write anything else?"

"Apparently George Eliot is a woman — at least that's what my English friend wrote when she sent me the book. She knows a lot of literary people. She said George Eliot's real name is Mary Ann Evans."

"Then why does she give herself a man's name?"

"It is considered improper for a woman to publish a novel. What nonsense!"

At that moment Aunt Priscilla stuck her

head in the front door. "Maggie, are you ready? I have your and Annie's lunches here." She held up a package wrapped in a towel. "And James said we could take you partway to school."

Mrs. Vanderpool looked up from her book. "Priscilla, dear, don't forget to see if there's any mail!"

Aunt Priscilla smiled. "No, Mama, we won't."

Two

During the years they'd been in Kansas, school in the small, one-room building had been for Maggie — most of the time — a source of discovery and delight. She would never forget how much their teacher, Miss Bailey, had helped her.

When twelve-year-old Maggie had first arrived from New York, she had been unable to read, a fact of which she was bitterly ashamed. But because of the long journey from Ireland, her father's death while working on the docks in New York, and then her mother's increasing illness, there'd been no time for her to attend school on a regular basis. Miss Bailey had been kind and sympathetic and tried to keep this fact from the other children. But then Miss

Bailey got sick and a substitute took over temporarily.

Maggie also never forgot the terrible morning when, thanks to the substitute, a Mrs. Smiley, it became obvious to the ten children sitting there that Maggie Lavin from New York couldn't read. It was after that that Mrs. Vanderpool, who up to this time had been brusque and distant, had helped her at home and given to Maggie her own love of books. Since then Maggie had done well in school and was one of the best readers.

This morning she was asked to read aloud from her essay on *David Copperfield*, and what they had all learned from it about English customs, particularly about poverty and orphans in Dickens's London.

A little nervous, Maggie stood up and read her essay aloud. Just before the final paragraph, she took a breath.

"It made me think about the time in New York when Annie's and my mother died and we were orphans on the streets, with no home. I came to see that being an orphan in New York was the same as being an orphan in London. The streets were lonely and frightening. When David was adopted by Betsey Trotwood he was finally not lost, but home."

"That's wonderful, Maggie," Miss Bailey said

when she'd finished. "You paint a very vivid picture."

But Annie often got into a little trouble, even with gentle Miss Bailey. During the geography lesson, centered on the Mississippi Valley, the teacher stopped and said, "Annie, we're supposed to be learning about the Mississippi, but I don't think you're even listening. What are you doing there?"

Annie hastily slid a paper under her reader.

"No, don't hide it, Annie! Come up here and show it to me!"

Annie sighed, got up, and slowly walked to the front of the class like a prisoner about to be executed.

Miss Bailey took the paper and looked at it. "This black kitten has nothing to do with the geography lesson, Annie. I'm surprised at you."

Annie looked down, then looked up again and smiled. "But drawing is so much more interesting than the Mississippi, Miss Bailey."

"It might be interesting if you knew more about it, which of course you would if you applied yourself."

Annie didn't say anything.

"Now go back and write me a page from your copy book on the Mississippi Valley and the crops that grow there," Miss Bailey said.

Annie didn't move.

"At once, Annie!" Miss Bailey was kind, but she wouldn't take disobedience.

"But I was drawing it for you, Miss Bailey. It's Blackie, one of Lilac's kittens. I thought you might want to take her."

"You had no business drawing that when you were supposed to be listening in class, Annie. Now go back and do as I ask. If something like this happens again, I'll have to keep you after school."

Maggie, watching her younger sister go back to her desk, felt a combination of embarrassment and admiration tinged with envy. If Miss Bailey had talked to her like that, she would be mortified and everyone would know it. But Annie was not in the least mortified: just stubborn. She's probably figuring out how she can wheedle that picture out of Miss Bailey later, Maggie thought.

She looked up to see Tom grinning at her from across the room. Quickly, she grinned back then glanced down, aware of her heart beating more rapidly.

Tom walked a part of the way back with Maggie and Annie. "Which just shows," Annie said later to Maggie, "how much he likes you." Tom lived a good distance on the opposite side of the school.

"That was good — what you wrote about *David Copperfield*," Tom said now to Maggie.

"You like *David Copperfield*, too, don't you?" Maggie asked. "I told Mrs. Vanderpool you did." Then, remembering the rest of her conversation with Mrs. Vanderpool about Tom, she blushed.

"Yes. Although I think that girl in the book, the pretty one, what's her name? — Dora — is sappy."

"Tom!" Maggie sounded half shocked, half amused.

He grinned. "Well, you know what I mean. I liked Agnes a lot better."

Maggie bent down and pulled a cornflower from the field. "These are so pretty. And there's one of your daisies." And she stooped and picked that, too.

"Why do you say 'your daisies' like they were different?" Tom asked.

"Because they are, different from the ones we had in Ireland. The ones here are bigger."

Tom looked at her. "But you're *here* now." He said it almost angrily. "I mean, you don't want to go back to Ireland?"

"No," she said, and blushed again.

They found Aunt Priscilla and Uncle James had returned when they got back to the cabin.

"How was town?" Maggie asked.

23

Uncle James didn't answer immediately. It crossed Maggie's mind that he looked a little upset. Then he said briefly, "Fine." He glanced at her. "Do you have an uncle named Michael Casey?"

It was like a hand touching her from across the world and far in the past. "Yes," she said. "He is — was Ma's brother."

"I see. Did he live with you in Ireland?"

"No. He was working in Dublin. We saw him when we went through on the way to Liverpool to get the boat. Why? . . . How did you hear about him?"

Uncle James held up a letter he was carrying. "When I picked up the mail I got this. It's from the Children's Aid Society in New York, the ones that sent you out on the train, along with the other children. They enclosed a letter from a Michael Casey who came over recently from Ireland." Uncle James paused. "He says he's your uncle."

There was a brief pause.

Maggie felt a trickle of fear and sadness. She wasn't quite sure why she felt afraid, but she was sad because mention of Uncle Michael made her think of Ma. "Did he say anything else?" she asked after a minute.

Uncle James put the letter down on the table near the cabin door. "He says some of the Irish immigrants down where you and Annie used

24

to live in New York told him that his sister had died and that you had been sent on a train to be adopted by a family out west. So he had gone to the Children's Aid Society on Astor Place and been told that it was true, they'd sent you two out to Kansas." Uncle James looked at Maggie. "He says he'd like to see you again and wants to know if we could send you back to visit him."

There was a fairly long pause, then Aunt Priscilla said gently, "I'm afraid we can't afford that. The Society never said anything about sending you back — even for a visit. Although, of course, they've sent an agent each year since you came to make sure you're happy and well treated." She paused and looked at Maggie. "Do you want to go back, Maggie dear?"

Maggie suddenly understood why she'd felt that touch of fear. "No," she said without hesitation. "I mean, if Uncle Michael wants to come here, we'd love to see him. But I don't want Annie and me going back there." She paused, and then when no one spoke, asked a little anxiously, "Was there anything else, Uncle James?"

"No." Uncle James picked up the letter and put it in his pocket. "I'll write to him tonight and send it when I go into town again."

The years out here had gone so fast, Maggie thought. She and Annie were happy now and the Russells were wonderful. But still painful was the memory of her mother's ravaged face when she was being put into the horse-drawn ambulance from Bellevue Hospital.

Aunt Priscilla was looking at her. "What is it, Maggie?" she asked.

"I was just thinking about Ma being put into the ambulance and how she looked. She'd had the sickness from when we were in Ireland. But it got worse. She knew she was dying, Aunt Priscilla, and talked about what happened to girls left alone in New York. That was why when a doctor from Bellevue knocked on the door asking if there were any sick children inside, she told him she wanted Annie and me to go on the orphan train." Maggie's eyes filled with tears.

Aunt Priscilla put her arm around her. "I'm sorry, darling," she said.

"It's all right. Since Ma had to die, I'm glad we're here."

Uncle James said, "You never talked about it before — I mean about the doctor from Bellevue. You told us about your mother's illness, of course."

"There were so many who died that way," Maggie said slowly. "The tenements were filled with them."

Uncle James cleared his throat. "Well, I know Priscilla's glad you're here. And you've been wonderful in helping out with her mother." He paused. "I'll write back to your uncle this evening and take it in tomorrow."

That night, when Maggie was lying in bed next to Annie in a corner of the main room, she heard from the Russells' bedroom Aunt Priscilla say quietly, "James, I know we signed the papers from the Children's Aid Society, when Maggie and Annie came to us. But did you ever see the lawyer about our legally adopting them? I remember you said you were going to after the first year."

There was a silence. Then Maggie heard Uncle James's voice. "No, I meant to. But other things always seemed more urgent."

"Is the lawyer in town now?"

"No, there was a note on his door saying he was out on his circuit."

"I see."

There was silence for a minute, then Annie suddenly whispered, "Mag, did Ma say anything about Uncle Michael? I mean, what he was like?"

"She always said he was sort of scholarly, like a poet. I think he worked for a paper in Dublin."

"Do you remember him, Mag? I mean, from when you saw him in Dublin?"

"Yes. He took us down to the dock."

"Did he look like Ma?"

"No. He was tall and thin. Ma had brown hair. His was sort of light and I think he had gray eyes — or maybe Ma said he did."

There was a short silence. Then Annie said, "Didn't Ma say he had a dog named McGuire?"

"I'd forgotten about that. Yes, she did."

As Annie turned over and curled up for sleep, she yawned and said, "I wonder what happened to him."

"Uncle Michael?"

"No. McGuire."

"Did you read Uncle Michael's letter?" Annie asked Maggie a day later before school. She was busy milking Bessie, and Maggie had gone out to get some milk for Mrs. Vanderpool's breakfast.

"Yes," Maggie said. "Uncle James let me read it and the letter from the Society it came with last night after you went to bed. The Aid people said Uncle Michael had come into their office wanting to know where we were and carrying an Irish newspaper saying that the whole orphan train idea was a plot to change Catholic children into Protestants by sending them to Protestant families."

Annie stopped milking for a moment. "That's not true!" Then, as the big cow turned her head, she said, "It's all right, Bessie," and started milking again. "Did they tell him where we were?" she asked Maggie.

"No. They just wanted Uncle James and Aunt Priscilla to know what had happened, and they enclosed that letter from Uncle Michael."

"Is he going to come out here?"

"He can't, if he doesn't know where we are and the Aid people won't tell him." Maggie stooped and dipped her pitcher into the milk bucket.

"Don't you *want* him to come out, Mag?"

Maggie looked at her sister. Annie sometimes astonished her. "No. It'd be nice to see him, but not if he's going . . . going to cause trouble."

Annie didn't say anything for a minute. Then she surprised her older sister again. "Mag, do you think Ma's getting Uncle Michael to do this?"

"What are you talking about? Ma's dead."

"I know that, Mag. She's with the Blessed Virgin. But they don't like the Blessed Virgin here so maybe Ma's getting Uncle Michael to come and take us back."

"Annie —" Maggie stopped, startled at the feeling of guilt that went through her. She knew that in moments of stress she often found herself silently saying a Hail Mary, something she felt Aunt Priscilla would understand, but was sure that Uncle James would not. But she'd never said anything about it to Annie because it had been harder for Annie to leave New York than for her.

They had come out to Kansas because it was Ma's dying wish for them. There were no Catholics here, so Maggie had made herself accept the plain service and vigorous hymns of the Baptist Church, which was attended by everyone in the small community. She had not forgotten her religion — she knew she never would — but it had become part of another life, a life she and Annie had had to leave.

Now Annie's innocent comment had brought it back. Because Annie was so much younger and had entered into the Sunday school's activities so enthusiastically, Maggie had assumed that she had forgotten her early years at Mass. Now she realized, with a shock, this was not true. She looked down at Annie, who was finishing her milking. "I didn't know you still thought about the Blessed Virgin."

"Oh, yes. I pray to her every night."

"I hear your prayers all the time and I've never heard you."

Annie stood up, pushed her stool away, and picked up the bucket of milk. "I don't pray aloud to her with the other prayers, Mag. I was afraid you'd tell Uncle James and he'd tell

Brother Evans and then he'd yell about me in his sermon."

Maggie was hurt. "Annie, you know I wouldn't do that!"

They walked back to the house. After a minute Annie said, "I wonder if Blackie is a boy or a girl. Aunt Priscilla said you can't tell until they're older."

Maggie recognized the tactic: Annie didn't want to talk any more about the Blessed Virgin. Maggie felt reproached. But she knew that to force Annie to do something she didn't want to do was next to impossible. "What about the other three kittens Lilac had? What are you going to name them?"

"Well, since I promised them to Sarah, Jane, and Jessie, I guess they'll name them."

Maggie thought about the conversation as she sat in Sunday school the following Sunday morning before church.

Sunday school was conducted in two rooms built onto the side of the wooden church. The larger room served both for Sunday school for the older children and whatever grown-ups wanted to attend and then, after church, when tables were put up and chairs placed around them, as a place to have the church lunch. The smaller room was used for Sunday school by the younger children, now being taught by a young woman recently arrived from the East. Covered dishes, brought by the women of the church, were warmed on the stove in the larger room throughout the morning in preparation for the midday meal.

Maggie, seated in the larger room, listened idly to Brother Thomas, the assistant pastor, who was teaching her Sunday school class. She was also intensely aware of the glances of some of the other girls as Tom made a point of coming over and sitting beside her. But her mind kept drifting away to her conversation with Annie about the Blessed Virgin. She wasn't quite sure what she thought about it. She knew that people out here held strong views on the subject of church and what people believed. But then so did people in the Five Points section of New York, telling Uncle Michael that placing children with families further west was a Protestant plot.

"What are you thinking about?" Tom whispered.

"About how angry religion sometimes makes people," she whispered back.

He grinned. "It's supposed to make people love each other."

"What are you two talking about?" Brother Thomas asked. "You should be listening to the lesson."

Tom hesitated, glanced at Maggie, then said,

"Just how it's funny that religion is supposed to make people love each other, but really makes them mad at each other."

Brother Thomas hesitated. "Well, it's necessary to defend what you know to be the truth."

"Yes," said Dr. Prendergast, who was sitting quietly in the back. "But whose truth?"

Maggie grinned.

"There's only one truth," Mrs. Smiley said, the corners of her mouth turned down.

"That's what all the sides say," Tom replied.

Mrs. Smiley turned. "If you don't watch out, young man, your soul will be in danger."

"Let's get on with the lesson," Brother Thomas said quickly. "Now about the parable of the loaves and the fishes . . ."

"Well, Annie," Uncle James said as they rode home in the wagon after Sunday dinner following church, "how was Sunday school?"

He and Aunt Priscilla were sitting up on the driving seat behind Rumpkin, the large gentle horse they'd had since Maggie and Annie had come to live with them. Maggie, who didn't have Annie's great devotion to all animals, nevertheless had a particular affection for Rumpkin and sometimes rode him. Maggie and Annie were in the back of the wagon.

"Mrs. Williams talked about the Good Samaritan and how dramatic it is and what a wonderful play it would make. She had some of us get up and act it out. Joe Blair was the man who was going to Jerusalem to pray and got attacked, I was one of the thieves and Steve Walker was the Good Samaritan."

"Are you telling us that you and Steve and the others *acted*?"

"Yes, Uncle James, it was wonderful!"

"I'm going to speak to the Elders," Uncle James said a little sternly. "One of the things we don't want out here is any nonsense about the theater."

"James," Aunt Priscilla said gently, "there's surely no harm in acting something out of the Bible."

"Uncle James —" Annie said, her voice rising.

"We don't want that out here," Uncle James went on as though Annie hadn't spoken. "We're starting clean and fresh to build a better society and we can't have anyone bringing in that sort of nonsense. I can't understand Brother Evans allowing it — that is, if he knew about it."

"It's not wicked," Annie protested. "I just imagined I was there on the road to Jerusalem, hiding behind bushes so I could jump on rich people who rode by —"

"They don't have bushes in the Holy Land,"

Uncle James snapped. "Anyway, you're too young to know what I'm talking about, but I'm not going to allow either of you to get mixed up in that kind of immoral behavior, and by the time I've finished talking to the Elders they'll feel the way I do. I'll wager Brother Thomas had something to do with this. He's not as strict about some things as he ought to be. And he was the one who suggested Mrs. Williams as Sunday school teacher."

"But she said she'd acted in New York and they did Shakespeare and good things like that, Uncle James. Don't you remember when Mrs. Vanderpool read *The Merchant of Venice* to us one night? And she said she'd seen —"

"Annie." Aunt Priscilla turned and put her hand on Annie's shoulder. "Let's talk about it later."

"But —"

"Later," Aunt Priscilla said firmly.

Annie closed her mouth, but she remained mutinous-looking. After a minute Maggie put her arm around her shoulder and pulled her sister to her. "It'll be all right, Annie," she said.

Annie grumbled under her breath, "How do you know there weren't any bushes in the Holy Land? What about Moses's burning bush?"

"What?" Uncle James asked.

Maggie glanced down at her sister.

"What about Moses's burning bush?" Annie said defiantly.

"That's different," Uncle James said. "It was a . . . a miracle."

Three

The second letter arrived three days later.

Maggie knew something was wrong when she and Annie got home from school. Annie had gone straight to the barn where Uncle James was busy getting hay to feed Rumpkin and Bessie. Maggie went into the house to help with dinner.

As she took off her bonnet and went toward the stove she caught sight of Aunt Priscilla's face. "Is something wrong?" she asked.

Aunt Priscilla sighed. "Uncle James picked up another letter from the Children's Aid Society. It seems your uncle Michael found out where you were sent. The man who wrote said he — your uncle Michael — somehow got the information from somebody working there who's new. Or maybe a friend of his did. Or he bribed somebody. Anyway, the man who wrote said he's pretty sure your uncle's on his way out here."

Maggie stared at her. "Can he . . . can he do anything?" A quiver of fear went through her. For the first time since she and Annie had come out to Kansas she felt their life here was under some kind of threat.

Faced now with the prospect of their mother's brother coming here, possibly to remove them, almost certainly to raise a fuss, she was aware again of how much this had become home, how deeply she had come to love the Russells, and how greatly she did not want to leave. "Can he, Aunt Priscilla?" she repeated.

"I don't know, Maggie dear. I certainly hope not." Aunt Priscilla glanced up, her blue eyes worried. Then she leaned forward and hugged Maggie. "I hope not," she said again. "Not if . . . not if James and I can prevent it — and you don't want it either, do you?"

Maggie hugged her back. "Of course we don't. We love you. You know we do."

"Yes, I know you do, though sometimes I wonder about Annie."

"She loves you, too, Aunt Priscilla! You can't have any doubt about that!"

"No. I know she does. It's not that. It's . . ."

"It's what?"

Aunt Priscilla hesitated. "Annie was

younger, of course, and adjusted very quickly. But I sometimes wonder if . . . well, if New York, the city itself, and . . . and everything she knew there somehow had more of a hold on her than it did on you."

"How could it? It was horrible!" Maggie protested. "I've told you how awful it was. With pigs rooting around the streets and garbage piled high and filth and waste being thrown out the windows and the scummy water in the gutter . . ." Then, "It always smelled so awful!" Her voice trailed off.

Aunt Priscilla grasped her hand. "Maggie darling, you don't have to think about that now."

As Maggie blinked back tears, her conversation with Annie about the Hail Mary sprang to her mind. She said slowly, "Aunt Priscilla, what did you mean, New York has more of a hold on Annie than on me? She was only seven when we left!"

"Yes, I know. Maybe it's because she was younger. The things you've told me about that were so terrible for you, the dirt, the smells, not having enough money, the manners of the rich folk — they might not have been so terrible to her. What she used to talk about were that little dog, what was his name? Timmie, and Mrs. O'Gorman."

Maggie smiled a little. "And the Green Harp

39

where Mrs. O'Gorman served behind the bar. Do you remember the fuss at church when Annie mentioned the Green Harp and everybody knew it was a saloon? I thought Brother Evans would have a fit."

"Yes, so did I."

Maggie and Aunt Priscilla looked at each other and laughed.

Aunt Priscilla said slowly, "What were you thinking about, Maggie, when you asked what I meant about New York still having a hold on Annie? You looked troubled."

Maggie hesitated. Then, "Annie and I were talking about Uncle Michael . . . something she said . . ." She glanced at the woman who had always shown such kindness and understanding. "Please, Aunt Priscilla, I don't want Uncle James to — to know this."

"What is it, Maggie? You know I can't promise that until I know what it is."

Maggie took a breath. "Annie . . . Annie told me when she says her prayers she still says, but not out loud, the Hail Mary. And — and sometimes I do, Aunt Priscilla, when I'm upset."

"My dear child, of course you do, you grew up with it and were taught it by your mother." She put her arm around Maggie. "There's nothing wrong with that. But, I do agree, it's better not to tell Uncle James, kind and wonderful as he is about so many other things. Or anyone else here."

Maggie hugged her again. "I'm so glad we came here. We were lucky."

"We were the lucky ones." Aunt Priscilla's voice shook a little. "And I do hope —"

"But can Uncle Michael do anything? I mean . . . I couldn't help hearing you talking to Uncle James the other night after we'd gone to bed. You asked if he'd seen the lawyer, and he . . . he said he hadn't had a chance. I know lawyers travel around . . ." Her voice trailed off.

Aunt Priscilla hesitated, then said, "One of the problems out here is that this town is too small to have a full-time lawyer. There's one who travels around some of these little towns. His name's Daniel Pierce and I've met him once or twice at church. But with his only being here occasionally, and James not being able to go into town during the worst of the winter or in planting or harvesttime . . ."

Maggie felt a queer sense of foreboding. "Then maybe Uncle Michael could . . . could make us go back," she said quietly.

"Maggie, don't think that. We'd never let that happen!"

Maggie was staring at her anxiously when Annie burst in, followed by Spot. "Blackie's caught a mouse!" she said excitedly. When she didn't get any immediate response she said, "What's the matter?"

After a minute Maggie said, "Uncle Michael might be coming out here."

"Oh? How wonderful!"

There was a silence, then Aunt Priscilla said, "Annie, why don't you come over here? I want to measure you and Maggie so I can cut the goods I got in town."

Annie ran over. "Let's see what colors you got."

Aunt Priscilla unwrapped a package. "Here, Annie, this blue-flowered print is for you. Maggie, I hope you like this lavender print."

"I love mine, Aunt Priscilla," Annie said.

"Mine's lovely, too," Maggie agreed and, finding herself wondering how Tom would like it on her, turned a bright red.

"I wonder what, or rather *who*, you're thinking about," Mrs. Vanderpool said, limping out of her room to join the others.

"I bet she's thinking about Tom," Annie said, and giggled.

"I'm not!" Maggie protested. Then, knowing she was lying, felt her cheeks go pink again.

"What's this I overheard about your uncle coming out here?" Mrs. Vanderpool asked.

Aunt Priscilla, getting a tape measure out of her sewing bag, said, "It seems like the girls' uncle Michael Casey is coming out here to see them."

"Hmm," Mrs. Vanderpool said. She glanced around at the faces and then went over to her chair near the table where she sat and helped out with some of the mending.

While she was being measured Annie said, "Aunt Priscilla, why does Uncle James think acting's wicked?"

Aunt Priscilla hesitated, as though choosing her words. Then, "Your uncle James came from a strict New England family, Annie. They had very high principles, which was why he volunteered for the Union Army to fight for Emancipation. But . . . well, sometimes people who are very strict and follow their principles disapprove of the way some of the people in the theater conduct their lives — and sometimes of the things that go on on the stage."

Annie looked up. "What things?"

"Well . . . sometimes they — the women on the stage — don't wear enough clothes when they dance around . . ." Aunt Priscilla's voice stopped.

A little while later, when Aunt Priscilla finished measuring Annie, she said, "You've grown. I knew you had, but I didn't realize how much." She straightened. "And now would you go out and bring some potatoes in? Maggie, come here and let me measure you."

43

"And you've grown, too, Maggie," Aunt Priscilla said a few minutes later. She glanced up from the tape measure and smiled. "You're almost as tall as I am."

At that point a bellow sounded from the crib where William had just awakened.

"Do you want me to see to him, Aunt Priscilla?" Maggie said.

Aunt Priscilla sighed. "Yes, would you, Maggie? He probably needs changing, and then I know he wants his dinner. I'm afraid I haven't had a chance to get a plate ready for him. Could you do that?" She smiled. "I sometimes think he thinks you're his mother, anyway."

Maggie went into the bedroom and, bending over the crib, picked William up. He stopped crying and put his arms around her neck. Then a happy, chortling sound came from him.

"All right, William," Maggie said, bouncing him as she carried him. "You're a fine big boy and a wonderful little brother!"

Annie, peeling off the skin from the last potato, looked up. "I bet you have lots of children," she said. Then added, "When you marry Tom."

"Annie!" Maggie could feel her cheeks get hot. "Now stop that! He hasn't even asked me yet! And anyway, I'm just fifteen."

Annie put the potatoes into a pot of boiling

water. "Elmira Higgins got married last month and she was fifteen."

"She was sixteen," Aunt Priscilla said. "But I'll grant, Annie, she only had her birthday a week before."

"Lots of the girls in Five Points were fifteen."

"Annie," Maggie said. "You were only seven when we came here. How can you remember something like that?"

"Because when you were up at Stewart's selling matches and there wasn't any school I'd go with Eileen and Patty to the church when somebody from the parish was getting married."

"I'm surprised Father O'Mara didn't chase you out!"

"He didn't see us, Mag. We'd squeeze down on the kneelers at the back so he couldn't see us and hear us giggle. We had *wonderful* times!"

Without thinking, Maggie glanced at Aunt Priscilla, remembering what she'd said about Annie and New York.

"Annie," Aunt Priscilla now said gently, "do you miss New York?"

Annie's cheeks went bright red. Taking a big spoon, she started stirring the stew pot. "I love you and Uncle James a lot," she said.

"I know you do, Annie dear. But that isn't answering my question, is it?"

"Sometimes I dream about it."

"You never told me that." Maggie, putting a spoonful of food into William's open and eager mouth, glanced up. "You never said anything."

"Sometimes I don't remember until we get to school, and then I forget before we get out of school. Aunt Priscilla, may I take a little of this leftover meat to Spot and Lilac?"

"It's not left over, Annie," Maggie said. "We can put it in the outside shed and use it tomorrow."

"No," Aunt Priscilla said, smiling. "It's not really left over in the sense that it would be thrown out. But yes, Annie, you may take it out to Spot and Lilac."

Uncle James, coming in the door, said, "So Lilac will not have as much motive to catch mice and rats as she might have if she were hungry."

"Uncle James, how would you like it if the only time you got fed was when you were so hungry you had to go out and hunt?"

"When we first came out here that was nearly always the case." He hung up his hat. "But you can take that out to the critters if you really want to," and his eyes twinkled as he smiled.

"Thank you," Annie said. She picked up a plate from a shelf under the sink.

"As I can see you were all prepared to," he said drily.

Annie suddenly gave one of her smiles, "her blinding smile," Brother Evans had once described it, half in admiration and half in disapproval. "You be careful how you use that smile when you're older, young lady!" he'd said. "Heaven knows what trouble you could get a young man into."

The next day Uncle James went into town to see if by any chance Daniel Pierce had returned. When he came back he told the others that the note saying he was away on business was still pinned to his door.

"Did he say when he'd get back?" Aunt Priscilla asked.

"No. I asked at the general store next door. But they knew no more than the note said. We're just going to have to wait until Dan gets back."

"I hope that's before the children's uncle gets here," Aunt Priscilla said.

"So do I," Uncle James replied gloomily. "I left him a note under his door, but there's nothing more I can do."

* * *

It was four days later when they were finishing supper that Annie, who was facing the window, said, "There's a man hitching his horse to the post."

Aunt Priscilla glanced out the window. "I wonder who it is."

Maggie turned around. Then she jumped up and ran to look out.

"Who is it, Maggie?" Uncle James asked.

In a voice that shook a little Maggie said, "It's . . . I think it's Uncle Michael."

Four

They were all at the door when the man walked up.

"Uncle Michael," Maggie said.

The tall, lean man took off his wide-brimmed hat, revealing thick, tawny-colored hair and gray eyes. His face was thin, with angular features.

"Maggie!" He took the hand she was holding out. "I'd have known you anywhere — even if I'd bumped into you on a street. You're that like your pa!"

Annie gave a little jump. "Uncle Michael!"

He looked down and smiled. "And you're little Annie?"

Annie gave her wide smile. "Yes."

He took both the hands she was holding out. "And you're like your ma." He looked up.

Maggie said quickly, "And these are Aunt Priscilla and Uncle James Russell, who have been so kind to us."

Uncle Michael shook hands with Uncle James and Aunt Priscilla.

"Come in," Uncle James said. "We were just finishing supper. But there's plenty left."

"You must be hungry," Aunt Priscilla said. "You've probably been riding all day. The nearest train station is hours away."

"Yes, the train arrived around eight this morning. I hired a horse to ride here." He glanced out the window. "She's not young and she's been carrying me for six or seven hours. Could I beg some hay for her and perhaps a rest?"

"Of course," Uncle James said. "I'll unhitch her and take her to the barn."

"Are you sure I can't —" Uncle Michael started.

"Oh, no," Uncle James said. "You stay here and have a bite. I can see Priscilla is already getting something ready."

"Do sit down, Mr. Casey," Aunt Priscilla said, putting some vegetables, potato, and boiled chicken on a plate. "I hope you like chicken."

"I do indeed, Mrs. Russell. Thank you. Maggie, Annie, come sit here so I can look at you."

Aunt Priscilla put the plate down in front of him. "May I offer you some coffee or milk?"

"Coffee would be grand, thank you."

He took a bite of chicken and potato and chewed and swallowed it. "That was good," he said. "Very good. Do you grow your own food, Mrs. Russell?"

"Yes, we do."

"You're lucky people here. The people back in Ireland would give much to have food like this."

"But the famine is over, isn't it, Uncle Michael?" Maggie said.

"The blight has gone, Maggie, thank God. But the landlords are still sending all our meat and wheat and other grain to England and selling it at a great profit. But let's not talk about that now. Tell me about yourselves since you've been here. Do you go to school?"

"Oh, yes," Annie said. "Maggie's one of the top readers in the class. And there's a boy who likes her very much."

"Hush now, Annie," Maggie said and felt herself redden.

At that point a scream rose from the Russells' bedroom.

Aunt Priscilla rose. "That will be William, announcing that he's hungry. Please excuse me."

Maggie half rose from her chair. "Would you

like me to feed him, Aunt Priscilla?"

"No, child. You sit there and talk to your uncle."

As she was going toward her room Mrs. Vanderpool's door opened. "Did I hear aright? Is that the girls' uncle from Ireland?"

"Yes, Mama. Let me get William and then I'll help you get ready for bed."

Maggie got up. "Mrs. Vanderpool, this is Uncle Michael."

Using her cane, Mrs. Vanderpool limped over.

"How do you do?" she said rather coldly.

Uncle Michael, who had also gotten up, bowed a little. "How do you do?"

Maggie smiled at the older woman. "More than any of the teachers, Mrs. Vanderpool helped me to learn how to read properly and has lent me books. That's what we always talk about, books."

"I am delighted to hear about it," Uncle Michael said. "But I'm surprised, Maggie, that you didn't know how to read when you came here. How old were you? Twelve?"

"Yes, but Uncle Michael, I'd barely started school in Ireland when we went to New York. Then I went to school there. But Ma got so sick and needed looking after, and there was no one to watch over Annie . . . So when I got here and went to school, I didn't really know how to read."

"Maggie's one of the really top readers now!" Annie said.

Uncle Michael smiled. "And what about you, young lady?"

Annie grinned. "I like to read. I love fairy stories, and stories about animals. But I'd rather draw than read."

"Please sit down," Mrs. Vanderpool said, "I'm just going to help Priscilla with William." And she limped toward the Russells' bedroom.

"I didn't realize they had a child," Uncle Michael said in a lower voice. "I thought they didn't have any."

"They didn't have any when we got here three years ago," Maggie said. "I think William was as much a surprise to them as anyone. But he's like our little brother, Uncle Michael! Isn't he, Annie?"

"Yes. Except nicer."

Uncle Michael laughed. "Why is that?"

"Because I remember little brothers of my friends back in Five Points and some of them were terrible. Always screaming and teasing animals and hurting them. I once saw some bully boys trying to set fire to Timmie's tail. William will never do that."

"That was cruel and disgusting," Uncle Michael said. "Was Timmie your dog?"

"No. He was Mrs. O'Gorman's."

"Ah, yes. I met her. I went with some friends

to the Green Harp. When I told her I was coming out here to . . . to see you she told me to give you her best wishes, and she said Timmie would send his, too, if he knew."

Uncle James came back in. "That mare is rather old," he said. "And hungry. She seemed grateful for the feed."

Aunt Priscilla came out of the bedroom holding William. "All right now," she was saying, "you'll get your dinner. Maggie, could you hold him for a moment while I heat up his meal?"

Uncle Michael watched while Maggie got up, took William from Aunt Priscilla, and sat down with him again. "William," Maggie said, "I want you to meet Uncle Michael," and she turned him to face her uncle.

William laughed and reached out his hand to Uncle Michael. "Uuuhn," he said.

"I think he's saying 'Uncle,' " Maggie said.

Uncle Michael smiled and shook his hand formally. "It's a grand boy you are! And healthy."

"Is there any reason he shouldn't be?" Mrs. Vanderpool asked, limping back into the room.

Uncle Michael turned. "I'm sure not, Mrs. Vanderpool. If I sound, well, more surprised than you would be it's only because so many of the children I have seen do not look as . . . as robust."

54

"You mean in Ireland."

"And to some degree in New York, among those who have arrived more recently."

"I take it conditions are not good for the immigrants in New York," Uncle James said. "Especially for the children. Isn't that why the Children's Aid Society started the orphan train? Because there were so many homeless children? And no one seemed to be doing anything about them?"

There was a silence. Then Uncle Michael said, "The Church did all it could. There are orphanages, but they have more than they can handle. I'm afraid there's little money, and it only goes so far."

After a brief silence Aunt Priscilla said gently, "You must be tired after that long journey. May we offer you a bed?"

Uncle Michael gave a weary smile. "Ay, I'd be grateful." He glanced around the cabin. "But where —"

"We thought you might not mind sleeping in the loft in the barn," Uncle James said. "It's warm enough, you'd have more than enough room, and the hay makes a softer bed than you'd get in the cabin."

The next day was Sunday. The morning sun, just coming up, poured through the window. Uncle James had gone to the barn. Annie was busy washing her face. Maggie was helping Aunt Priscilla fix breakfast and set the table.

"I was thinking of asking your uncle to join us at Sunday school and church, Maggie," Aunt Priscilla said. "I assume he's a Catholic, so I hope he won't be offended."

Maggie, slicing the bread, stopped. "I don't know, Aunt Priscilla. I mean, I remember him from Dublin. But only just from seeing him. Ma did say once —" She stopped.

"What did your mother say, dear?"

"I'd forgotten 'til now. She said once that Uncle Michael was thinking of studying to be a priest. But he mustn't have, because when we saw him in Dublin, Ma said he was working on a paper — I've forgotten the name. But it was something to do with the independence movement."

At that moment Uncle Michael appeared in the doorway to the cabin. "Good morning, Mrs. Russell, and Maggie and Annie," he said.

"Good morning, Uncle Michael," Maggie said, and smiled at him. Even though he was fairer than Ma and didn't really resemble her, there was something about his face and features — and certainly his voice — that made Maggie think of her.

Uncle Michael strolled over to the table, his eyes on Maggie's face. "Why are you sad, Maggie?"

She paused. "I didn't know I was sad. I guess I was thinking about Ma."

"Ah, she was a lovely girl, your ma, Maggie. Especially when she was young — perhaps your age now. What are you? About fifteen?"

Maggie smiled. "Almost sixteen."

"And," Annie said, coming around the small screen behind which she had been dressing, "Tom Brinton is sweet on her."

"Annie!" Maggie said, embarrassed.

Uncle Michael smiled. "And who may this young man be?"

"He's a boy in my class, and Annie exaggerates." Maggie looked at the floor.

At that moment Uncle James came through the door carrying a bucket of milk and some eggs in a small bowl. He gave the eggs to Aunt Priscilla who broke them into a pan on the stove, and poured the milk into a pitcher which he then put on the table.

A few minutes later Aunt Priscilla said, "Everybody come and sit down and we'll have breakfast."

They all sat down. Uncle James said grace, and, after a pause, offered thanks for Uncle Michael's safe trip across the country.

"Uncle Michael," Annie said, "what happened to McGuire?"

"Ach, Annie. He got killed. He was a good dog!"

"That's sad. I'm sorry." She paused.

"Did you meet Spot when you were out in the barn?"

"I did, indeed. A proper guard dog he is, but Mr. Russell introduced me, so we're now friends — at least I hope so."

"He's a wonderful dog, Uncle Michael," Annie said. She glanced sideways at Uncle James. "Sometimes I'm allowed to let him in here, aren't I, Uncle James?"

"You know I don't think animals should be allowed in the house," Uncle James replied. He smiled at Annie. "But I'm not always as strict about it as I ought to be."

"Would you like eggs, Mr. Casey?" Aunt Priscilla asked.

"I would indeed, Mrs. Russell."

As Aunt Priscilla put eggs and browned potatoes on his plate she said, "When did you arrive here — I mean in New York?"

"About two months ago. I knew some of the people who work on the *Irish World* and hoped to get a job on the paper."

"Did you succeed — in getting the job, I mean?" Uncle James asked.

"Ay. I did, and found a room off Broadway, near Baxter Street."

"That's part of Five Points, isn't it?" Maggie asked.

"Ay, it is."

"That's where we used to live," Maggie said.

"Yes, I know. I knew where you had lived because your ma had written to me, before she got so ill. When I arrived and went to inquire as to what had happened to you, some people there told me about your mother's illness and death and that Children's Aid had sent you out here."

"Ma wanted us to come," Maggie said. "She was the one who asked the doctor who came by where the Children's Aid was and where she could send us to get on the train."

"Ay, one of your neighbors, a Mrs. O'Brien, said she knew Margaret — your mother — had wanted you to do that."

There was a brief silence. Then Aunt Priscilla asked gently, "Do you think she was wrong, Mr. Casey?"

Uncle Michael didn't answer for a moment. Then he said, "There was an article in the *Irish World* that said the main reason for the children being sent out of New York was to turn them from their faith — to make them into Protestants. And I know many people in New York — and in the Church — believe that."

"That's nonsense!" Uncle James said. He sounded angry.

"Is it, Mr. Russell? Please don't be offended. I have only been here a short time, but long enough to see how well Maggie and Annie look and what kindness you have shown to them. But have they been to Mass in the three years since they arrived?"

Uncle James opened his mouth but was stopped by Aunt Priscilla, who put her hand on his arm. "Mr. Casey, I understand how you must feel. But there are no Catholic churches out here. Most Catholics west of the Hudson are, I think, in cities — St. Louis or much further south in New Orleans. The children who were sent out went to farms and small towns. The Children's Aid Society was very careful where they placed them, and went to great trouble to send out agents beforehand to investigate the families who said they would be interested in adopting any. And they have sent an agent each year since Maggie and Annie arrived to make sure they were being treated well."

"Uncle Michael," Maggie said. "They've been wonderful to us!" She turned to her younger sister. "Haven't they, Annie?"

"Yes, Uncle Michael," Annie said. "They have."

"I can certainly see that," Uncle Michael said.

There was silence. Then Uncle James said, "We know you wanted to see your nieces, Mr. Casey. You wrote asking us if we could send them back. But even if we were willing, we couldn't afford that. And where were you planning to have them stay?"

There was a pause. Then Uncle Michael said, "I thought I might speak to the sisters —"

"Uncle Michael," Maggie said. "You saw what it was like for young girls in New York. If she was lucky, a girl could be a maid in some grand person's house. If not — well, the other thing a girl could do — well . . ."

"Ach, Maggie —" Uncle Michael ran his hand through his hair. "Of course not — but you mustn't forget your own religion, your heritage!"

Uncle James said angrily, "A heritage of drunks and illiterates who rioted in the streets of New York and hanged helpless Negroes!"

"Uncle James!" Maggie and Annie said together.

"James, please!" Aunt Priscilla said. "That's a dreadful thing to say!"

Uncle James, whose face had flushed, paused and took a breath. He drew his hand across his forehead. "I'm sorry! But I'll never forget back when we — the Union troops — marched to New York to quell the draft riot and I saw a black man hanging dead from a lamppost. And all because the Irish were too cowardly to fight in the war!"

Uncle Michael said carefully, "I've heard

61

about the draft riots. There are many Irish in New York who feel as distressed about what happened as you. As for being illiterates — the Irish had centers of learning and teaching for centuries before there were any such schools in England."

"I'm sure what you're saying is true," Uncle James said, "and I apologize again for my rudeness." He paused and added emphatically, "But Maggie and Annie belong here now."

After another pause Uncle Michael said, "I should go out and see to my horse."

"I gave her some hay and feed," Uncle James said, "and I thought while we're at church we could turn her loose in the field behind the barn where I let Rumpkin graze. That is," he looked directly at Uncle Michael, "unless you have other plans involving her."

"She could probably do with a graze," Uncle Michael said. He glanced at Aunt Priscilla. "And what church would that be?" he asked.

"It's a Baptist church," Uncle James said.

"We'd be delighted to have you go with us," Aunt Priscilla said.

Uncle Michael looked across the table at her. "I take it Maggie and Annie will be going to church with you."

"Yes. As they usually do," Aunt Priscilla replied.

There was another pause. Then Uncle Michael got up. "You're very kind, but I think perhaps I might take a walk around the country here. It's very beautiful, very fertile, grand farming country." He smiled. "I will see you later, then."

When he had gone Uncle James got up and said, "We have to get moving or we'll be late."

Maggie, shocked and hurt by what he'd said, burst out, "I didn't know you felt that way about the Irish, Uncle James. You've never said *anything* like that before."

"Maggie, I've already apologized twice," Uncle James said testily.

Maggie looked at him for a minute, then got up.

Aunt Priscilla glanced at her husband, hesitated, but said nothing.

Annie, who hadn't moved from her chair at the table, suddenly burst into tears.

"Annie dear," Aunt Priscilla said. "You know Uncle James wasn't talking about you."

"But *I'm* Irish," Annie said, sobbing.

Aunt Priscilla turned. "James —"

"I've already said — oh, Annie, I'm sorry. I didn't mean it. I really didn't! I wasn't even thinking about you!" He leaned over her and put his arms around her shoulders. "You know how much your aunt Priscilla and I love you, Annie!"

Maggie, watching, smiled ruefully.

Aunt Priscilla looked across at Mrs. Vanderpool. "Mama, are you coming to church this morning?"

"Not this morning, my dear. I'll stay and look after William, if you want to leave him."

"I'll help you with your bed," Maggie said, following Mrs. Vanderpool into her room.

They were busy with the bed when Mrs. Vanderpool said, "Maggie, don't let yourself be too upset by what James said. You must know he's devoted to you and Annie."

"I've always believed that . . . that he loved and . . . and wanted us here," Maggie said.

"Well, of course he does. He loves you very much."

"But what he said about the Irish in New York . . ." Her voice trailed off. "How he and Aunt Priscilla felt about Annie and me . . . always meant so much! . . . Now —"

"You have to remember he was the young man who volunteered in the army because he felt so strongly about Emancipation."

Maggie smiled and relaxed a little. "Yes, he did, didn't he?" But inside her there was still pain.

Five

Later at Sunday school, Mrs. Williams said
crisply, "It seems my idea of acting scenes from
the Bible is considered wrong by some of our
members. So of course we won't be doing it
again."

"I liked it," Annie said. "I liked doing it a lot.
I thought it was a wonderful way to show what
happened."

A boy behind her put his hand up. "So
did I."

Annie's friend Sarah said, "I did, too. It made
it real."

There were more murmurs of agreement.

Mrs. Williams said, "Well of course I liked it,
but you must know, Annie, that it's your
guardian, James Russell, who brought up the

objection. He seems to think acting is the way of the devil."

A loud murmur started. "That's silly," one of the other children said. "I think it's a wonderful idea. I told Ma and Pa and they thought so, too."

"I shouldn't have said that," Mrs. Williams said guiltily. "Mr. Russell has as much right as anyone else to say how he feels." She hesitated, then went on, "It's just that — to me — it's such a hidebound way to think."

Maggie, sitting across the room among the older children, heard the exchange and was torn. She agreed with Mrs. Williams that Uncle James was being hidebound and she was still angry and hurt at what he'd said earlier that morning. But she still felt great affection and loyalty to him and to Aunt Priscilla for the love and care they'd shown Annie and her.

After the service she and Tom sat together on a bench behind the church talking about Uncle Michael.

"Why do you think he's come, Maggie? Is it to try and get you to go back with him?"

"I guess so, Tom."

Tom reached out his hand and clasped Maggie's. "I don't want you to go, Maggie."

She looked at him. "You don't, Tom?"

"You know I don't. I have plans . . . I know

it's too soon. But Dad was talking . . . when we graduate he wants me to go to college."

"That would be wonderful for you, Tom. Don't you want to go?"

"Sure, but that means I'm gone four years. I won't see you except in the summer. And I don't want someone else making time with you when I'm away."

Maggie blushed a little. "You don't?"

"No, I don't. So I won't go unless we . . . we have a sort of a . . ." He squeezed her hand. "An understanding —"

He stopped abruptly and snatched his hand back when one of his friends, Eric Steirs, came up and said to him, grinning, "They're really going at each other around the front."

"Who?" Tom asked.

"Why, your dad and James Russell. It all started with Mrs. Williams having her class act a scene, and James Russell now saying he thinks it's a sure way to the devil and your dad telling him he's a boneheaded idiot." His grin widened. "Brother Evans is trying to keep them apart."

After he walked off, Tom said, "Maybe I'd better go and see what's going on. Dad can get awful mad sometimes."

"I'll go, too," Maggie said. She felt awkward. Tom's father had been a Confederate officer during the Civil War and Aunt Priscilla had once said something about the two men having different viewpoints about the war. She had added, "But out here we try to let the past stay in the past."

They heard the voices before they got around to the front of the church.

"That's a lot of puritanical rubbish," Paul Brinton was saying angrily. "In the days before you all decided to come and straighten out the South we used to have troupes with some of the great plays — *Hamlet, Macbeth,* and others — come through Virginia, and people'd take their children to them."

"If it's just Shakespeare or some of the other great playwrights, there's nothing wrong with that," Uncle James replied heatedly. "Nobody's opposed to that. But it doesn't stop there. After the Shakespeare players, the next troupe coming through will likely as not have naked women on the stage and who knows what kind of story about adultery or any other immorality. Then everybody wants to go to it, including young people, and it's too late to draw the line."

"Of all the lamebrained —"

Tom, who had walked forward, put his hand on his father's arm. "Dad —"

Paul Brinton, a tall, fair, handsome man, turned angrily, but when he saw it was his son he paused. "All right," he said. He looked back at James Russell. "If you think it's all right for the children to be illiterate as long as they're moral, then do it your way."

"It's still better than the way they were in your part of the country."

Brinton, who'd been turning away, swung back. "And what does that mean, pray? In what way was my part of the country less moral than yours?"

"Having slaves is not exactly setting a high moral tone. We had to teach you a lesson about that, didn't we?"

Brinton's fist shot out and caught James Russell off guard. Uncle James reeled back and was prevented from falling only by some of the others standing around.

"Dad!" Tom pleaded, his hand on his father's arm.

"Why you —" Uncle James had recovered quickly. His arm went back. The next thing Maggie knew, Paul Brinton was lying on the ground, quite still.

Aunt Priscilla clasped her hands around her husband's arm. "No, James, please. Not here. That's not right."

Brother Evans stepped in front of him. "Mrs. Russell's right, James. This is the church and it's Sunday." He turned then and looked at Mr. Brinton, who was being helped to his feet by Tom. "You shouldn't have done that, Paul,"

Brother Evans said. "We're all out here to try and heal the past."

"If that sanctimonious —"

"Dad, please," Tom said.

Paul turned to his son. "There's such a thing as family loyalty," he said.

Tom hesitated. Then, "I know, Dad. You don't have to remind me."

"Then remember it, son."

For a moment Tom and his father, who were almost the same height, looked at one another. Then Paul Brinton strode away, followed in a second or two by Tom.

The dinner served afterward was subdued and the two Brintons — Mr. Brinton was a widower — did not attend. Only Mrs. Smiley made reference to what had happened. "It's a pity that people from certain parts of the country don't know how to behave," she said, taking an overly large bite of apple pie.

Maggie, watching, saw the narrow, ill-tempered mouth for once filled out and found herself wondering what Mrs. Smiley had looked like when she was young.

After an uncomfortable silence, Uncle James said, "I shouldn't have said what I did." He glanced at his wife. "I'm sorry, Priscilla."

"Then why —" Mrs. Smiley started.

Dr. Prendergast turned toward her. "Let's change the subject, shall we?"

She opened her mouth, showing still, Maggie noticed, some apple pie.

"Right now."

There was a chorus of "Yes, let's."

Mrs. Smiley closed her mouth and went on chewing the apple pie.

When they got home, Uncle James, who had not spoken on the way, went to unharness Rumpkin and turn him loose in the small field behind the house he'd planted with grass specially for him, where Uncle Michael's horse was happily nibbling away.

Aunt Priscilla, Maggie, and Annie went into the house. Uncle Michael was sitting in a chair reading. He had pulled William's crib over and with one hand was rocking it.

Aunt Priscilla looked surprised. Then she went over. "Has he been crying?"

"A bit," Uncle Michael said. "But he quieted down." He glanced over at his niece. "Reminded me of Maggie when she was a baby. I used to look after her sometimes before I took off for Dublin."

Aunt Priscilla lifted William out of the crib. "You're getting to be a big boy," she said. She touched his face. "You're a bit hot, aren't you?" Her hand felt William's bottom. "And you need changing. Maggie —"

"Annie and I'll start fixing supper, Aunt Priscilla," Maggie said. She looked around for Annie, and saw her sister disappearing across the back toward the barn. "Or anyway, I will," she added under her breath, then reflected that in some ways it was easier to do chores without Annie than with her. It wasn't that Annie was unwilling or unable to get out the dishes and set the table. But sometimes — even often — Annie's hands would slow down while her fantasies soared. She called them the stories in her head. A waste of time and nonsense, Mrs. Smiley had more than once described them, an opinion echoed by some of the other women when Annie had been caught gazing out at the fields when she should have been busy helping them clean up after church dinner.

But at that point Mrs. Vanderpool limped out of her room and started helping Maggie with the vegetables.

"How was church?" she asked.

"We missed you," Maggie said. "Mrs. Evans asked after you."

Mrs. Vanderpool grinned a little. "That was charitable of her. She thinks I'm well down the primrose path."

"What's that?"

"The primrose path?"

"Yes."

Uncle Michael suddenly spoke up. " 'The

primrose way to th' everlasting bonfire.' In other words, Maggie, hell."

Maggie chopped for a while, then asked, "Where does that come from?"

"From *Macbeth,* I believe," Mrs. Vanderpool said. "Am I right, Mr. Casey?"

"You are, indeed."

"Do you like Shakespeare, Mr. Casey?"

"Ay, I do. He was a great poet and playwright."

"What are you reading, Uncle Michael?" Maggie asked.

"It's Irish poetry, written in Irish. Can you remember any of it at all, Maggie?"

"Just a few words. Ma would talk in it sometimes."

"It's almost dead in Ireland, Maggie. That was one of the things the famine destroyed."

Mrs. Vanderpool looked over at him. "How could a famine, terrible as it was, I'm sure, destroy a language?"

"Because, Mrs. Vanderpool, it destroyed the people who used it. A million died, you know, and another million left, either by emigration or being transported."

After a short silence Mrs. Vanderpool said, "And did Mrs. Prunes and Prisms want to know why I wasn't in church, Maggie?"

Maggie grinned. "Yes. And Aunt Priscilla said you weren't feeling well."

"Did she believe her?"

Maggie finished slicing the potatoes and put them into a pot of water. "I don't know. I guess so." She stopped. "There was . . . there was . . . well, something happened after church."

Mrs. Vanderpool looked up. "What?"

Maggie described the quarrel between Paul Brinton and Uncle James.

"Hmm," Mrs. Vanderpool said. "Paul Brinton may be a fellow Southerner, but he ought to watch his tongue and his fist. It's true that James can be . . . well . . . strict." She paused. "The trouble is . . ."

Maggie looked up at her. "What?"

"He's inclined to hold onto it. His anger, I mean."

The next morning at breakfast, Maggie had cause to remember what Mrs.Vanderpool said about Uncle James and his anger.

He said suddenly, "Maggie, I was thinking about what happened. I'd prefer you not to have anything to do with Tom Brinton. He and his father hold very different views from us on . . . on important subjects."

"James —" Aunt Priscilla said.

"I mean what I say, Priscilla, and I don't want to discuss it." And he got up from the table and went out.

"But —" Annie started.

"Later, Annie," Aunt Priscilla said.

When they got to school Maggie knew immediately that the other boys and girls had been talking about what had happened after church, because they all stopped the moment she and Annie arrived. She prayed no one would say anything to either of them. As she sat down, she glanced quickly at Tom, but his eyes were on the open book on his desk. Feeling let down, she got her things ready for class.

Mrs. Gresham, a new arrival in the community, was substituting for Miss Bailey, who was away. When she introduced herself on her first day in the school, she said she had taught in Kentucky, where she and her husband came from. Maggie prayed that Mrs. Gresham wouldn't say anything. But, as she had learned, not all prayers were answered the way she wanted them to be.

The class had barely begun when Ellen shook back her gold curls and held up her hand.

"Yes, Ellen?" Mrs. Gresham said.

Ellen got up. "We were talking before school and some of us think this'd be a great time to have a discussion about the War and slavery and so on, don't you think so, Mrs. Gresham?"

Mrs. Gresham hesitated only a few seconds. "Why, yes, Ellen, I do think that's a good idea. Does the rest of the class agree?"

A chorus of yeses followed, punctured by one loud "no" from Tom and a quieter one from Maggie.

"I think you're outvoted, you two. Whatever they are, things are better when aired. Why don't you say what you think, Ellen? We can hear from Tom and Maggie later."

"Well, slavery was wrong, everybody knows that, but my dad says that the South was beaten not because it was wrong, but because it was outnumbered, even though the soldiers were braver and fought better."

"I see. Well, does anyone else have anything to say, either to agree or disagree?"

There was a silence, then Gertie Bates, one of Ellen's cronies, said, "My ma says she was in Jackson, Tennessee, when the Union troops came through, and they stole everything they could get their hands on — jewelry, silver, everything. They were all of them thieves." She turned. "Don't you think so, Tom?"

Tom said in a curiously flat voice, "Most armies feel entitled to take from the people they're fighting against."

"But your daddy fought for the South." Ellen sounded scandalized.

Tom looked at her. "Soldiers are soldiers. Some will steal and some won't. It has nothing to do with which side's right and which isn't."

"Well, I think it's terrible how the South was

put down and defeated, when everybody knows the Southerners were braver."

Tom smiled suddenly and said, sounding more pronouncedly Southern than Maggie had ever heard before, "Why we thank you, ma'am, for those kind words. It's nice to know somebody feels that way."

He didn't glance at Maggie, yet she felt, somehow, that the words were directed at her.

The class laughed. Mrs. Gresham smiled. Ellen blushed and then giggled and nervously twitched, one golden curl falling to her shoulder.

"Maggie Lavin," Mrs. Gresham said unexpectedly, "what do you have to say about this?" As Maggie stared and then started to speak, the teacher added, "Stand up when you address the class."

Maggie stood and found herself thinking that Tom hadn't been told to stand up. She pushed that thought away and said, "I was living in Ireland when the Civil War was on, at least most of it, Mrs. Gresham. Me da and ma and Annie and me didn't come over until it was almost finished." As though her voice belonged to somebody else she heard the pronounced Irish in it, and realized she hadn't talked that way for a long time.

Mrs. Gresham shook her head. "I, Maggie, I. 'Annie and I didn't come over until after the war.' You know better than to talk that way now."

Ellen, who had not sat down, shook back her hair. "The Irish in New York were too busy burning and looting to bother about helping free the slaves. James Russell was there when it happened. He said it was enough to make you sick. He said —"

Maggie turned suddenly and ran out of the schoolroom and kept running right over the low hill behind the school and on. She ran as long as her breath lasted. Then she slowed and stopped and finally threw herself down on the ground. Around her the tall grass waved. After a few minutes she put her hands over her face and only when she felt the wet on them was she aware she had been crying.

After a while she lowered her hands from her face and stared at the ground. But instead of the long blades of grass she saw Tom's face when he smiled at Ellen and heard the tone in his voice when he spoke to her. Tom — who had always been scornful of Ellen's many tricks to make him notice her, who had criticized her for the mean things she'd said . . .

She closed her eyes and heard in her mind his voice, sounding like his father's, drawling and Southern. She had always known Tom's family had come from the South, but it had never been important. They had been friends for at least two of the three years she had been here in Kansas, and she'd never heard him sound like that. She knew his father had fought for the Confederacy, because once when the class had visited the Brinton household, she had seen a huge flag nailed over one wall and asked whoever was standing next to her what it was.

Again it was Ellen who, overhearing her question, answered. "That's the stars and bars, Maggie. Don't you know? That's so strange. There was this terrible war and you don't even know the flag the Confederacy fought for."

Maggie had asked her question in a low voice. Ellen's had been in her most carrying tones. No one could have missed it. And no one did.

"It's right funny you don't know about the war, young lady," one of the older people standing around had said disapprovingly. "Don't they teach you anything in the school out here?"

Tom had said, "Well, Ellen, if you went to a European country where they'd just had a civil war, would you know which flag belonged to which side?"

"I'd make it my business to know, Tom." And

then her face had broken into her most entrancing smile, all her dimples showing. And Tom had smiled back.

One of the things Maggie noticed was that when Ellen smiled that way, most of the grown-up males standing around always had something nice to say. Even some of the women.

What had that priest in St. Andrew's Church, back in Five Points in New York, said? In his homily at Mass he stated that God always answered prayers. Having watched her mother cough up blood that morning, she had accosted him after Mass and said angrily she didn't believe him. She had prayed and prayed for God to make her mother better, and He hadn't.

"Now, Maggie," the priest had said. "I didn't say He answered prayers exactly the way you wanted Him to. But however terrible the circumstances you can always get some good out of it. It's your job to find out how. Now say three Hail Marys for forgiveness for doubting Him."

And, of course, because of her mother's illness and death, she and Annie had come out here, which was what Ma had wanted.

Maggie slowly stood up and realized from the color of the sky that some time had passed since she'd run out of the schoolhouse. What time was it? she wondered. The thought of Tom crossed her mind, and the words he had said when they were sitting outside the church seemed now to taunt her. She pushed them away angrily. The South was wrong, she thought, with a passion that surprised her. It had enslaved black people and tried to hang onto them. Uncle James, who volunteered for the Union Army because he believed in Emancipation, was right. Never before had she felt it this strongly —

Then, like a clear rebuke, what he had said Sunday morning echoed in her mind, calling the Irish in New York drunks and illiterates who rioted in the streets and hanged Negroes . . .

Uncle Michael had said many of the Irish in New York were themselves distressed about what had happened. And no matter what he said, or didn't say, she was sure he wanted her and Annie to go back with him.

Never before since she had been here had she felt so torn. New York, the city itself, seemed to loom nearer. As for the Civil War, always before it had been a struggle that had nothing to do with her. Now —

Slowly she got up and wiped her face with her handkerchief. When she got back to the school the others were coming out for lunch. Suddenly she saw Tom emerge from the door.

Before she could stop herself, she called, "Tom!"

She knew he heard her because he looked in her direction. For a second their eyes met. Then he turned away and said something to the person on the other side of him. She moved a fraction, and saw it was Ellen. Ellen looked straight at her, then looked up at Tom and the two of them resumed talking.

Others in the class looked at her. One or two seemed on the point of speaking, but didn't. For a moment Maggie felt as alone as she had in New York, and as unwanted as she did when she and Annie came out here among people who were so different and who seemed to look down on everything she and Annie were. Automatically her eyes searched for Annie among the younger students and spotted her with two or three others. Annie saw her at that moment and came over.

"Where did you go, Maggie?" she asked. "I almost went with you, then I knew old Gresham'd just stop me if she could, and anyway make a big fuss."

"I just went outside for a bit," Maggie said, and by automatically belittling it to Annie, felt the pain inside her diminish a little.

Maggie realized her lunch was inside the schoolroom with her jacket, but she wasn't eager to go back in. Mrs. Gresham was obviously still in there and would certainly demand an explanation from her.

"Would you like to come eat with us?" Annie asked.

"No thanks, Annie. I — I have to go inside for something." Nobody of her own age had approached and Maggie's sense of isolation increased. Then she saw Rachel Schmidt coming toward her. Rachel's family had recently moved from Illinois and before that from Germany. Knowing how it was to be a stranger, Maggie had made a point of being friendly toward her.

"It's too bad what happened, Maggie," Rachel said. "I know how you feel."

"Do you?" Maggie said. For a minute Tom's image was clear and prominent in her mind. Then again she pushed it away. "I thought I'd forgotten how people feel about the Irish, how they look down on them, but then something like this morning happens and I know I haven't forgotten it, I won't ever forget it. Maybe I — Annie and I — should go back East with our uncle. At least in New York you know where you stand!" She was astonished to hear herself say that.

Rachel stared at her a minute. "Please don't do that. You've been very nice to me. People don't understand. My parents talk with a funny accent. They don't talk like other Americans out here and I know people sometimes make fun of them. The other kids are just embarrassed about what happened with you and Tom. They don't like Ellen, either."

But talking about what happened with Tom was too painful. She and Tom had been known to be friends, almost — in the teasing words of some people at church — sweethearts. And now he had publicly humiliated her.

Afterward Maggie couldn't remember the rest of that day at school. She and Annie had walked home almost without talking. As they got near the house Annie said suddenly, "Mag, what are you thinking?"

"What it would be like back in New York."

"I don't think you'd like it back there, Mag. Where would we live? In Five Points? And have you forgotten, Ma wanted us to be here."

Maggie didn't say anything.

"Is it because of Tom?" Annie asked.

"It's because of what Ellen said about the Irish, Annie. That's the way a lot of the rich people talked in New York. I remember Ma, when she was working in a house, coming home and telling us some of the things people said about the Irish. Terrible things, with her standing there, waiting on table, and them knowing she was Irish. I didn't think anybody out here where everybody comes the same way would talk like that."

Annie didn't say anything.

Six

"I told you not to have anything to do with young Brinton," Uncle James said angrily when Maggie had managed to give an account of what had happened in the school.

"That's hardly the point, James," Aunt Priscilla said gently. She had her arm around Maggie's shoulder and was patting it.

"Well, I certainly won't have anything to do with him anymore," Maggie said bitterly. "He didn't stick up for the Irish in any way when Ellen was going on about the riots and what thieves and villains they were —" She caught sight of Uncle James and stopped abruptly.

Annie went up and put her arms around Maggie's waist. "Ellen was just being a beast because Tom always liked you better," she said.

"Not anymore," Maggie said bitterly. "And anyway, I don't care. He can . . . he can like anybody he wants. I'll have to see him in school and church, I suppose. But I'll not pretend we're friends anymore."

Mrs. Vanderpool opened the door to her room and limped in. "You know, I took William into my room with me and I think he has a slight fever," she said.

Aunt Priscilla turned immediately and went into Mrs. Vanderpool's room with her. She bent over her mother's bed where William was lying on his blanket and felt his face and neck. "You might be right," she said slowly to her mother.

Maggie, hearing her, went in. It seemed to her that William's round face was a shade more flushed than usual. At that point he started to cry fretfully. Aunt Priscilla picked him up and started singing to him softly and rocking him a little in her arms. He continued crying for a while but finally quieted down and was put back in his crib in the Russells' bedroom.

Nothing further was said about the episode between Uncle James and Mr. Brinton. Maggie was silent. Every now and then Aunt Priscilla would look across at her and once or twice seemed on the point of speaking, but evidently decided not to.

As they sat down to dinner Aunt Priscilla

glanced up at Uncle Michael, who had just entered the house from outside. "Mr. Casey, please join us."

Uncle Michael smiled. "That'll be kind of you." He sat down between Annie and Mrs. Vanderpool.

"Have you made friends with Spot, Uncle Michael?" Annie asked. "Does he come into the barn with you?"

"Ay, he's a good dog — and now seems to accept me as a friend." His gray eyes seemed to twinkle. "Y're like yer ma, Annie. She grieved something awful, I'm told, when you couldn't take yer dog with you to Liverpool."

"I remember that," Maggie said suddenly, breaking her silence. "He kept running behind the wagon on the road. Ma wanted to stop and take him up, but Da wouldn't."

"You wouldn't have been allowed with him on the boat," Uncle James said.

Uncle Michael glanced at him. "Happen you're right," he said.

"What part of Ireland do you come from, Mr. Casey?" Mrs. Vanderpool said.

"Well, I've spent the last ten years in Dublin, but before that we were in County Meath."

"Maggie tells me you worked on a paper in Dublin."

"Ay, *The Nation.*" He added, "It's for independence for Ireland."

After a short silence Mrs. Vanderpool said formally, "It's a beautiful country."

"You've been there, ma'am?"

"Yes, I stayed in Dublin when I was a girl. My mother and I were visiting friends there."

"It's also a sad country, too, Mrs. Vanderpool."

"Yes. We saw that."

The next day Uncle Michael said, "I'll be walking to your school with you both, Maggie."

"All right," Maggie said. She dreaded returning to school and was quite determined that neither by look nor word would she acknowledge Tom's existence. He was Ellen's friend now. And, Maggie thought angrily, she could have him.

"Do you think you'll be able to find your way back?" Uncle James asked Uncle Michael.

"We'll show him the landmarks," Maggie said, smiling a little.

They walked for a while. Maggie pointed out a hill here, a sudden hollow there that could be used as markers.

"It doesn't look that way at first," Uncle Michael said. "But I can see now, the land is rolling."

"When I first came out here," Maggie said, "it all looked the same, miles and miles of flat land. But after I'd been to school a few times

I saw that it's not flat at all. And then after that blizzard, when we got lost . . ."

"Spot saved us," Annie said.

"Surely, you weren't sent to school in a blizzard?"

"No, of course not," Maggie said. "It was fine when we set out, and if I hadn't been kept back by Mrs. Smiley and Annie hadn't been sent home alone, we'd have both been back before it really got bad."

"And Uncle James came in the wagon," Annie said, "but I'd fallen down and couldn't get up. Spot came to look for us and lay down next to me and kept me warm."

"And if he hadn't," Maggie said, "Annie would have frozen to death. Because the blizzard came up suddenly."

Uncle Michael looked down at Maggie. "Tell me, Maggie, wouldn't you like to come back to New York with me? From everything I could gather from the Children's Aid Society the Russells didn't formally adopt you."

"Uncle James meant to," Maggie said and found herself wondering if it were true. "It's just that lawyers out here travel from town to town. Aunt Priscilla explained the town's too small to have one here permanently, and when Uncle James could go into town, Mr. Pierce, the lawyer, was somewhere else." She paused.

"Surely if it meant enough to him he'd have

made a point of going whenever the lawyer was in town."

It was as though he was giving voice to her own doubts and fears, Maggie thought. But she said stubbornly, "It's not that easy if it's planting and harvesting time. And it does mean a lot to him." As she spoke she heard within her mind his comment about the Irish. Deliberately she pushed it away.

But inside she was torn and unhappy. Before that unpleasant episode at school she'd have vehemently denied any interest in going back. Now — she felt bruised and muddled and, for the first time in three years, perhaps unwanted.

Uncle Michael glanced at his older niece. "You were born and brought up Catholic, Maggie. It pains me to see you so far away from the Faith."

Maggie didn't speak for a moment. Then she said, "I don't think God is going to condemn everybody who isn't Catholic. If that were so, then Uncle James and Aunt Priscilla would go to hell. And I don't believe it."

"That's a complicated argument, Maggie —"

"And Ma didn't think so either, or she wouldn't have wanted us to come out here."

Uncle Michael didn't say anything and they walked in silence for a while. Maggie knew she had temporarily silenced her uncle. But it hadn't stopped the tug-of-war within her that went on as they walked the rest of the way.

After a few more minutes Annie said suddenly, "Miss Bailey's back! See, Maggie? She's over there, talking to Rachel."

"Yes, she is. At least that's something."

"Is Miss Bailey your teacher?" Uncle Michael asked, staring at the young woman surrounded by students.

"Yes, and she's wonderful," Annie said enthusiastically.

Miss Bailey left the others and approached Maggie, Annie, and Uncle Michael. Maggie found herself thinking again how pretty the young teacher was, with her thick chestnut hair and hazel eyes.

"Good morning, Maggie, Annie." Miss Bailey's eyes rested on the man beside them.

"This is our uncle Michael Casey from Ireland," Maggie said, "and this is our teacher, Miss Bailey."

"How do you do, ma'am," Uncle Michael said, bowing a little.

Miss Bailey held out her hand. "It's nice to meet you, Mr. Casey. Did you come to visit your nieces?"

"If truth be known —" Uncle Michael said, and then paused. "Well, yes, ma'am, in a manner of speaking, I did."

"He came to take us back because he thinks we're getting made into Protestants," Annie said.

"Well, now," Uncle Michael started. Then he smiled a little wryly and stopped.

Miss Bailey looked back at Uncle Michael. "Is that true, Mr. Casey?"

He hesitated a moment. "That's what the newspaper in New York said, ma'am. And many of the people — the Irish — in New York believe it."

Miss Bailey said, "There are no Catholics out here. But from everything I've learned, that was not the purpose of sending out orphans."

"No. Probably not." Uncle Michael sounded oddly depressed. "And my own family in Ireland could not have been kinder than Mr. and Mrs. Russell. And Maggie here and Annie are fine and healthy. It's . . . it's a problem."

"Would you like to come into the school and perhaps tell the children about Ireland? I know they'd be interested."

Uncle Michael hesitated only a second, then, "If you think it would be of use to them, ma'am, I'd be happy to."

He stood before them, a tall, lanky figure, seeming almost awkward at first. But he was really at ease, Maggie decided, as though he had addressed classes or groups of people before. She relaxed a little, and as she did so, realized how tense she'd been about him and how he would strike the class.

"Tell us about Ireland, Mr. Casey," Miss Bailey said. "We hear now and again about the trouble going on there when somebody brings a newspaper from New York, or a traveler like yourself comes."

"It's a terribly sad place now, Miss Bailey, even now, more than twenty years after the famine."

He paused for a moment. Miss Bailey looked around quickly, but no one seemed to want to ask questions, so she said, "We've heard of the famine, of course. Can you explain what it meant to the people?"

He cleared his throat. "The main food — often the only food — of the Irish is potatoes. In 1845 a blight, or disease, hit the potatoes and they all became black and rotten. That meant that a million farmers and their families who lived on the potatoes starved. That's why so many came to America, to get away from the terrible conditions and the starvation."

Miss Bailey glanced around the small schoolhouse. "Would anyone like to ask any questions?"

Ellen's hand went up. "But Mr. Casey, why don't the Irish eat something beside the potato? What about wheat or corn? Didn't any of that grow over there?"

"Indeed yes, but most — if not all — of it was exported by the landowners."

A boy sitting near the front, Willie Mc-Whorter, said, "Why didn't you stop them? Why didn't you drive them out?"

"That's easier said than done, son. The English have been occupying Ireland since the twelfth century. That's some seven hundred years. There is now, and there has been for at least two hundred years, an English army of occupation there, and under Cromwell, they, with their armies, laid waste to the land."

"My dad said Cromwell was a hero," Willie said. "He said his father came from Massachusetts and his family, going back to the colonial days, were pilgrims from England. He — my dad — said Cromwell drove the Catholic church and its . . ." he paused, obviously trying to remember the right words, "its weak-kneed cousin, the Church of England, out of the government, and put in the right faith."

Maggie's and Annie's heads turned. Maggie held her breath.

"Understandably," Uncle Michael said pleasantly, "the Irish view him in a different light." He paused. "In addition to the usual acquisitive motive that has carried the English around the world — including, of course, its former colonies in America — Cromwell had a religious purpose: He was a fanatic Puritan, determined to stamp out Catholicism in Ireland."

Uncle Michael paused and smiled. "But the notion that appears to be prevalent in America — that the Irish are illiterate savages — seems to me astonishing. And, incidentally, it's not true. In centuries past, when most English could hardly read or write, there were seventeen centers of learning in Ireland."

"That's a stinking —"

"Everybody knows the Catholics —"

"JUST A MINUTE! NOW EVERYBODY BE QUIET!" At the sound of Miss Bailey's cool but carrying voice all the other voices stopped.

"My goodness," she said indignantly. "I didn't realize what a fuss I was going to raise! I would like you all to remember that Mr. Casey came to speak to us at my invitation and I am ashamed to have to apologize for the rudeness that's just been shown him." She turned to him. "I do apologize. And I realize now I should have prepared them ahead of time."

He bowed a little. "I'm glad to have had the opportunity to speak."

Tom's hand went up.

"Yes?" Uncle Michael asked.

"I was talking to my father last night," Tom said. "He went to England when he was fresh out of college before the War Between the States and he was there while the famine in Ireland was going on. He said there were strong voices in the English Parliament — that's like Congress, I guess — wanting to do something about sending food to Ireland and helping out during the famine, but they couldn't persuade the others in Parliament."

"That's true. There were indeed voices, such as Sir Robert Peel and Lord Clarendon in Parliament, who wanted to send the Irish-grown food back to alleviate the suffering. But they were outvoted."

"But didn't the Irish own any land of their own?" a boy near the back asked. "I mean that they could grow their own food on?"

"I'm afraid by seventeen hundred, a little more than half a century before your revolution, almost all the arable land in Ireland was owned by the English, who differed from the majority in language, religion, and culture."

Ellen shook back her hair. "Why didn't the Irish have any famous writers like the English ones we're reading in class?"

Uncle Michael smiled. "Actually we have a great number, but most of them wrote in the Irish language. But among noted English writers were several who were actually born in Ireland: Jonathan Swift and the great playwright, Richard Brinsley Sheridan, among others."

He looked at the class. "You have schools here. I'm in one now, thanks to Miss Bailey's kindness. In Ireland we have what we call hedge schools, because they're held anywhere — in huts, barns, and under hedges — which a great number of Irish children attend and where, among other subjects, Greek and Latin are taught." He paused. "How many of you here are learning Greek and Latin?"

No hands went up. There was a silence.

"None, I'm afraid, Mr. Casey," Miss Bailey said wryly. "I think the Irish are ahead of us there. Please do go on."

"I've gone on too long, I'm afraid. You've all been very patient. But I feel I must add, finally, some words of Edmund Burke, an Irishman in the English Parliament — and a great friend of the American colonies, by the way.

"In writing of the Penal Laws, laws enacted by the English that criminalized the practice of Catholicism among the Irish, Burke described the laws as 'A machine of wise and elaborate contrivance, as well fitted for the oppression, impoverishment and degradation of a people, and the debasement in them of human nature itself, as ever proceeded from the perverted ingenuity of men.' " Uncle Michael paused, then, into the silence, he said, "Burke wrote, 'The aim was not the persecution of a sect, but the degradation of a nation.' "

There was a silence. Maggie found her hands clenched and herself near tears as pride in her uncle, in his knowledge and learning, filled her.

No one said anything. Uncle Michael turned to Miss Bailey. "I'd better be getting back now while I remember the way." He hesitated a moment. "And the best to you."

He looked over at Maggie and Annie. "I'll be seein' you back at the Russells'."

Maggie knew some of her friends were eyeing her a little nervously as though almost afraid to approach her, but she felt unable to break down whatever wall it was she had erected around herself since yesterday. Even Annie, it seemed, was outside that barrier.

"I thought Uncle Michael was fine in class today, didn't you?" Annie asked, as they walked home.

"Yes," Maggie said briefly.

"Ah, Mag, what are you so mad about? I mean, I know about the fight and Tom and everything —"

Maggie swung around. "I don't want to discuss that. Do you hear me?"

Annie stopped and stood where she was, watching her sister as Maggie walked on. After a minute or two Maggie stopped and turned. "Why have you stopped?"

"I don't want to walk with you when you're like this. I haven't done anything, but all you do is snap my head off."

Maggie turned around again and went on walking for a minute. Then Annie saw her stop and put her hands to her face. Annie ran up to her and put her hands on Maggie's arms. "I'm sorry, Mag! I know it's Tom and I'm that disappointed in him! But . . ."

Maggie put her arm around her. "No, Annie, it's I that am sorry. You've done nothing and I'm behaving like a shrew!"

They walked on. Maggie had her arm around Annie's shoulder. After a while Annie asked anxiously, "Are you thinking about going back to New York with Uncle Michael?"

Maggie said with a sob, "I don't know, Annie, I don't know."

Seven

On Sunday Uncle James brought out the wagon to take everyone to church. Aunt Priscilla had William on her lap. "He's still not quite himself," she said. "But I think the outing will do him good."

Uncle James, Aunt Priscilla with William, and Mrs. Vanderpool sat up front on the bench. Maggie and Annie sat on the floor of the wagon in back.

"That's your new bonnet, Mag, isn't it?" Annie said when they were going out to get in the wagon.

"Yes. Aunt Priscilla made it for me."

"The blue matches your eyes."

Maggie smiled, losing a little of the tension in her slender body. "You've been kissing the Blarney stone now, Annie. My eyes are gray, not blue. You're the one with the blue eyes."

As though reminded of his host's duties, Uncle James said formally, "You're welcome to come to church and Sunday school with us, Mr. Casey . . ."

"Ach now —" Uncle Michael started.

"But you must do as you think best."

"Why don't you come along for the ride," Aunt Priscilla suggested. "It's a beautiful morning." She smiled. "You don't have to come into the church. There's a small pond nearby. You can sit there."

"I might just," Uncle Michael said. He stepped on the wagon wheel hub and then into the back of the wagon. "It is indeed a beautiful morning."

As they rode off Aunt Priscilla glanced over her shoulder at Uncle Michael. "Do you have mornings like this in Ireland?"

"Ay, we do. A bit more damp, maybe. And not as warm."

They rode in silence for a while, making their way through fields of green corn and wheat sprouts. Uncle Michael said suddenly, "You have grand land for growing things. I can see why you came out here."

"There's Miss Bailey," Annie said when they drew near to the church building and saw the people standing around outside.

Maggie, who was watching Uncle Michael,

saw his eyes were on the teacher. Something in his gaze made her think he liked her.

"Well, here we are," Uncle James said. "The pond's over there under the trees. Please feel free to go where you want. And —" He stopped abruptly.

"And?" Uncle Michael asked. He was halfway out of the wagon, one long leg on the ground, the other still on the wheel hub. But he paused.

Uncle James gave one of his unexpectedly attractive smiles. "You do understand, I'm sure, that you may encounter some church members who'll feel impelled to try and convert you, or at least express their disapproval of your own church."

"Ay," Uncle Michael said, grinning a little, "I'm well aware of it."

Uncle Michael drifted over to where Miss Bailey was talking to Brother Thomas, the assistant pastor. Miss Bailey introduced them and the two men, after a moment's hesitation, shook hands.

"Emma Bailey tells me you're fresh from Ireland," Brother Thomas said.

"Ay, I am that."

"My mother's family was Irish," Brother Thomas said.

Uncle Michael looked at him. "Did they come from Ulster?"

"No. They came from Roscommon." Brother Thomas hesitated. "But when she married my father, who was of Welsh extraction, she — er — converted to his Methodism. Later they both switched to the Baptist Church."

"I see."

It seemed to Maggie that the two men were walking on eggs.

At that moment Tom Brinton and his father strolled around the corner of the church. Seeing the Russells they stopped.

Maggie's heart gave a thump. Then her mind was flooded with the memory of Tom's treatment of her during the past few days. Pointedly she turned away from the Brintons. "Uncle Michael," she said clearly, "would you like to walk down to the pond with me? It's pretty and there are some wildflowers growing around the edge."

Her uncle nodded. "A good idea."

Maggie couldn't see Ellen McCandless anywhere. As she and her uncle walked she prayed Ellen wouldn't show up. Her second and much angrier thought was that she didn't care if she did. Ellen was welcome to Tom Brinton.

And then, from nowhere, came a memory of a time when she and Tom were walking home after school. Annie had awakened with a cold and had been kept home that day. Tom lived in the opposite direction, but he went with

104

Maggie almost as far as the Russells' cabin. Nothing unusual happened. He cracked jokes. She laughed. He took her hand to help her over a muddy little stream that had sprung up suddenly and disappeared as suddenly a few days later. Then, when she was about to release his hand, he wouldn't let it go. "I like us being alone," he'd said, his face a little flushed. He added quickly, "Not that I don't like Annie. I do. But not the way I like you."

"Oh, Annie wins everybody's heart," Maggie said.

"Not everybody's," Tom said. "Not mine."

Maggie remembered feeling the heat in her cheeks and not knowing what to say. At the same time she felt an enormous happiness. So often people were drawn to Annie, with her dancing eyes and radiant smile. Then Maggie reproached herself for begrudging her sister people's admiration. But nothing mattered at that moment because of the way Tom was looking at her and the way it made her feel.

Maggie was suddenly aware now of the prick of tears behind her eyes. "Something eatin' at you, Maggie?" Uncle Michael asked.

"Nothing, Uncle Michael," Maggie said.

He glanced at her and then looked away. "Who was that pretty girl in school the other day, the one that I wanted to shake?"

Maggie gave a slightly shaky laugh. "Ellen. Ellen McCandless."

"Looked to me like she was out to make trouble. Why would that be?"

To her amazement Maggie heard her own voice. "Because she wanted Tom Brinton to like her instead of me." She hadn't put it that bluntly to anyone until now.

"Would that be the good-looking lad who talked about the English Parliament?"

"Yes. How did you know?"

"I don't know. Maybe because I saw the way Ellen looked at him. And I saw the way you did, too. He seemed educated — I mean more than most."

"His father graduated from some big eastern university and traveled to Europe. That was before the war, I guess. And he talks to Tom about all kinds of things, like history and what kinds of governments people have and so on."

"What was the fight about betwixt him and James Russell?"

Maggie told him, then added, "It's funny anybody as brainy and . . . and educated as Mr. Brinton would stick up for slavery."

"Ah, Maggie, it's my observation that people's opinions have more to do with how they feel than what they think. And when they know in their hearts they're wrong, they get all the madder. You can make a case for almost

106

anything. I suppose the English think they've made a case for all they've done in Ireland. The trouble is, the better educated and brighter people are, the more they believe their convictions come from pure thinking and right reason."

There was a pause as they reached the water's edge. Then Maggie sighed and said, "I heard Aunt Priscilla say something like that once."

"She's a good lady, Maggie. Make no mistake about it!"

"I know she is. She's wonderful." Maggie paused. "Uncle . . . Uncle Michael, are you still going to . . . to try and take Annie and me back?"

Her uncle turned and looked down at her, his gray eyes as bright as the sky. "I am, indeed, Maggie. One thing has nothing to do with the other. I'm a loyal son of the Church, and the Church doesn't waver about that. I have to make sure that you and Annie are returned to it. It's my duty!"

A chill touched Maggie. She let go his hand. "I have to go into Sunday school now, Uncle Michael."

For the Russells and Maggie, the church dinner after the service was a rather silent meal. As far as Maggie knew, Uncle Michael had not restated to the Russells his determination to take Annie and her back to New York. But they seemed aware of it, and also nervous about how the community would treat him at the dinner. During the meal, while people asked questions about Ireland, Uncle Michael kept his answers general and unchallenging. It was as though everyone had tacitly agreed to a hiatus of peace.

But when they got back later that afternoon, Uncle Michael turned and faced the Russells. "You've been kind and hospitable to me, and I am truly grateful for the kindness you've shown my nieces, giving them a home and care and affection. But —" he took a breath, "as I told Maggie at the . . . at your church, since there is no Catholic church near here, that doesn't mean it isn't my duty to take her and Annie back and return them to their own church."

"I'd think the Children's Aid Society would have something to say about that," Uncle James said, his voice cold and hard. "After all, we signed papers."

"But you didn't formally adopt them, did you?" Uncle Michael asked. "I asked a lawyer about this before I left New York and he told me that if you had adopted them in a court of law, then it'd be the same as if they were your own. But if you didn't, then those papers you signed with the Aid Society wouldn't stand up against a blood relation."

There was a silence. Then Maggie said, "But Uncle Michael, Annie and I don't want to go! What if we refuse to go with you?"

"Then I'll have you legally forced to."

"How can you talk like that?" Annie cried.

"It's my duty," Uncle Michael said almost pleadingly.

"This is our home," Maggie said. "And Ma wanted us to come here."

"She was dying, and probably wasn't clear in her head —"

"And it was you who said that . . . people don't act according to the way they think, but the way they feel," Maggie said passionately.

"If you are loyal to the Church —" He spoke desperately. Almost, she thought, as though he were trying to convince himself.

"You know," Aunt Priscilla said, "I have read the New Testament fairly closely, and I don't remember one occasion when Christ threatened force to make anyone believe Him — or believe in Him."

"But they're my nieces, my family, Mrs. Russell. My only family here."

There was a silence.

Uncle James took a step forward. "I am going to ask you now to leave our house, Mr. Casey. I don't know about your ways, but according to ours, you have violated our hospitality. Please go. Now. I'll have your horse ready for you. You can get into town before dark." He walked out the door.

It took Uncle Michael only a few minutes to thrust his garments into a saddle bag. Then he left without looking back.

Eight

"I'm going into town to see if Dan Pierce is back yet," Uncle James said the next morning after breakfast. "Annie, will you be sure to take care of Bessie before you go to school? Milk her and put her out to graze?"

"Yes, Uncle James." She looked at him for a minute. "Dan Pierce's the lawyer, isn't he?"

"Yes, he is."

Annie suddenly ran to him and flung her arms around her adopted father. "Oh, Uncle James, I do hope he says we don't have to go with Uncle Michael!"

The bearded man smiled suddenly and gave her a quick hug back. "So do I," he said, and then went out. Through the cabin window they saw him riding in the direction of the town.

As they were clearing up breakfast, Maggie said, "Aunt Priscilla, would you like me to stay and help you — seeing as how Uncle James won't be here to do his chores?"

"Thank you, Maggie. I don't think that'll be necessary." She glanced at the dark-haired girl. "You're not eager to go to school this morning, are you?"

Maggie sighed. "No, not really." She didn't say anything for a moment, then, almost passionately, "I can't wait for it to be over."

"You know," Aunt Priscilla said after a moment, "I wouldn't be totally convinced of Tom's apparent liking for Ellen McCandless. He's never liked her before."

"It's different now!"

"What I suspect is different is not how he feels about that girl, but the pressure his father is putting on him. Remember, Maggie, what Paul Brinton said to Tom? Something about there being such a thing as family loyalty?"

"Why should that make him act sweet to Ellen?"

"Didn't she say the Confederate Army was braver and fought better?"

"What she was trying to do was so plain —"

"Yes. To you and probably to most of the young people there and maybe even to Tom.

112

But he also may have been feeling under attack."

"Nobody was attacking him!"

"Maybe he was trying to convince himself!"

"I don't care what he does!"

"If that were entirely true, Maggie, you wouldn't be thinking about not going to school. A few times when you've felt isolated from the other children about coming from New York or being on the orphan train you've shown the same reluctance. Even if you haven't said so, I've known it."

To her own surprise and embarrassment, Maggie burst into tears. She stood near the sink, her hands over her face. "I didn't know I liked him this much," she sobbed. "It's awful. I almost wish I could go away." Looking up she saw Aunt Priscilla's face. "Oh, not to New York or with Uncle Michael. But . . . but . . ." She broke down again.

Aunt Priscilla put a hand on her arm, and then drew her into her arms. "It's hard. I know."

"Did you ever feel this way?" Maggie sobbed. "Oh, I know you love Uncle James, but I meant when you were young or . . . or . . . before Uncle James?"

Aunt Priscilla dug a handkerchief out of her pocket. "I'll tell you something if you promise never to tell anyone."

113

Maggie blew her nose and looked up at her. "Of course I promise."

"You know my family were all Southern and any who were involved in the army, or whose children were, were Confederates. I met James at the house of some Washington friends. He, of course, was in the Union Army and was there in uniform and most of the guests there stayed on the other side of the room away from him. Our host and hostess, who were from Washington, had lived in New England at some point and had known his parents. That was why he was there. Anyway, there he stood by himself with no one talking to him. I felt sorry for our rudeness, so I put down my teacup and went over to talk to him." She paused. "That's how we met."

"What happened?"

"What happened was that I fell in love with him and according to what he said later, he fell in love with me. But he was feeling ostracized, so while he was polite, he was stiff — you know how he can be sometimes — and left soon after. But I guess he felt he'd been rude or something. Anyway, a day or two later, I received a note from him, thanking me for my kindness and asking if he could call. That was the beginning. I wrote him back and told him yes. When I told my mother, she was furious. Anyway, he came. As I said, we fell in love, even though we couldn't do much but sit in our drawing room and drink tea. Finally, one time, I was sure he'd come to propose and I was determined to accept him, though my mother had said if I did she would throw me out of our home and wouldn't leave me anything in her will. I told her I didn't want anything. Anyway, James didn't propose when I thought he would. I could see he wanted to, but he didn't. I was pretty sure it was his pride because my family had so much more than his." Aunt Priscilla paused and absentmindedly ran her hand over a stain on the sink stand. "So I wrote a note and told him how much I wanted to marry him."

Maggie gasped. "Aunt Priscilla, you *didn't!*"

"Yes, I did."

"And he wrote back?"

She smiled. "He did better than that. He came in person. My mother was not expecting to see him, so when she came into the drawing room and found us holding each other's hands and kissing, she almost had a fit. She told him to leave instantly and told me to go to my room. I told her if he left I'd go with him. Mother said he was only doing it because my family had money. I told her I didn't care about the reason and if she didn't apologize to him, I'd leave anyway."

Maggie gazed in admiration at Priscilla Russell. "I think you were wonderful," she said. And then added, "But Mrs. Vanderpool is out here with you and Uncle James and they seem to get on fine."

"They're not kindred spirits, Maggie, but they've come to respect one another. And I think they're fonder of each other than either one will admit."

"But if your family had money, I'm surprised she came out here."

"We lost everything, Maggie. Our property was in the South, in Virginia and North Carolina. It was devastated by the war and of course the slaves were freed and there was no money to pay for labor, so it had to be sold. There was very little money left."

Maggie stared at her for a while. "But I know you think slavery was wrong."

"Of course I do. That has nothing to do with it."

They went on cleaning up. Maggie asked, "What do you think I ought to do, then, Aunt Priscilla?"

"Go on to school and try not to be too angry or too hurt. Tom's a nice boy. Even though I don't think he's behaving well right now, I'm sure he's having a bad time. The quarrel between the two men was one thing — after all it's natural they'd disagree. But his father had no right striking James that way. And then

116

his father talks to him about family loyalty."

"I suppose he's acting this way about . . . about Ellen because Uncle James is my adopted father."

"Probably, Maggie. I wish he wouldn't. But young people in love behave strangely — as you should know!" Aunt Priscilla gave her a brief hug. "Now go on to school!"

Maggie kept her eyes away from Tom as much as she could, which, in a small classroom, was not always easy. Pretend he doesn't exist, she told herself.

It didn't help when she heard Ellen's voice pointedly and loudly addressing him during the recess and the lunch hour.

At the end of what seemed like a long day she felt abnormally tired and her neck, which she had held rigid so as not to turn around and give even the appearance of looking for Tom, was stiff.

"I thought," Miss Bailey said as she was about to ring the bell, "we might start the custom of having a class picnic in the spring of the year, to celebrate the end of winter. And I decided next Friday would be a good day — if it doesn't rain!" Everybody laughed. "What do you think?"

"That's a wonderful idea," several voices said, Ellen's loud and clear among them. Mag-

gie, who normally would have been enthusias-
tic, thought avoiding Tom would be even more
difficult on a picnic than in the classroom. So
she said nothing. And though she strained her
ears, she couldn't hear Tom's voice until Ellen
said loudly, "Tom, don't you think that's a ter-
rific idea?"

"Yes. Wonderful." His tone was crisp and
curt. Maggie found herself wishing she could
see his face, but as he sat in the back, there
was no way she could without turning.

"Good, then," Miss Bailey said. "Everybody
bring something — sandwiches, bread, fruit,
cheese, cooked chicken. We can boil water
there and make coffee."

As they were streaming out of the school
room Miss Bailey said, "Maggie, may I see you
for a minute?"

"Wait for me, Annie," Maggie said.

"All right," Annie said resignedly. "But try
and hurry. I was hoping to walk with Sarah
and Deborah."

"If it's such a bother," Maggie said coolly,
"go on ahead. I can manage alone." She heard
her own tone, cold and unfriendly, and felt
sorry. It wasn't Annie's fault. But she felt tense
and irritated and was unable to do anything
about it.

When the others had left the classroom, Miss
Bailey said, "Maggie, the atmosphere today in

school was tense, as though everybody were on the edge of an explosion of some sort. I know — I've heard since I got back — that Paul Brinton and James Russell had a fight of some kind while I was away, but I don't like to see it spill over into the classroom. Did something happen here?"

Maggie, struggling for words that would not reveal how she felt, hesitated. Then, feeling the teacher's eyes on her, said, "I think Tom . . . Tom is trying to be loyal to his father. His father . . . Mr. Brinton told him to remember family loyalty when they had their . . . their fight."

"But that doesn't really explain why you so plainly feel as besieged as you do, Maggie."

"I'm not —" Maggie started, then caught her breath. "I'm not . . ."

"I'm not blind, Maggie. You and Tom have always been friends. Everybody's known that."

"Well, we aren't anymore, Miss Bailey. He's friends with Ellen now."

"I see. By the way, how's your uncle — Uncle Michael, I think you called him."

"He's . . . he's gone."

Miss Bailey glanced at her. "In peace or war?" she asked drily.

"Well . . . he said he was going to try and take Annie and me back to New York. He says it's his duty. Uncle James asked him to leave."

"Considering how kind the Russells have been —"

"He thanked them for that. But he said he had to get us back to the Church anyway. It's his duty and we're the only family he has over here." She paused. Then, "The funny part is, he'd just finished telling me that people who think they're acting out of their heads, aren't. They're acting out of feelings. But when I reminded him of that he said this was different!"

Miss Bailey hesitated. "Maggie, it's useless to try and make sense of how people act sometimes, particularly when their feelings or emotions are involved. Try to remember Tom's being loyal to his father."

"All right, I'll try," Maggie said.

When she went outside Annie was sitting on a small bench, waiting.

Maggie opened her mouth to say something like, "I told you to go on." Instead she said, "I'm sorry I was rude, Annie. Thanks for waiting."

Annie's angry look relaxed. "You were rude, Maggie, but it's all right."

When they got back to the cabin Uncle James was in the barn, in Rumpkin's stall, looking at his hoof.

"Is something wrong?" Maggie asked. She was fond of the big gentle horse.

120

"Seems to have injured his hoof. He was acting lame."

"What can you do?"

"Mostly, I think, let him rest. I'm not a farrier, but I don't think it's that serious, not if he rests it."

After a minute Maggie said, "Was Mr. Pierce there?"

"Yes."

"What did he say, Uncle James?"

"He said that as far as he knew the papers we signed for the Children's Aid Society had never before been questioned, but that he'd look up the law and write to the Children's Aid Society to see if they have any helpful information or ideas."

"Do you think it'll do any good?" Annie asked.

He glanced at the two girls. "We have to have faith it will. After all, it's in the Society's interest, too, to establish that they send out only children who otherwise wouldn't have homes and are without relatives to claim them. Your uncle Michael was certainly not there to take care of you."

There was a silence. "I'd better go in and help Aunt Priscilla," Maggie said.

"And tell her about the picnic," Annie added.

But Maggie didn't get around to mentioning the picnic until later, because when she got back to the cabin it was obvious Aunt Priscilla was upset about something. Both she and Mrs. Vanderpool were in the Russells' bedroom, bent over the crib.

"What's wrong?" Maggie asked, coming up behind them. "Is something the matter with William?"

Mrs. Vanderpool turned. "I'm afraid his fever is up."

"He was all right this morning," Maggie said. She loved William as though he were her younger brother. "I fed and bathed him before breakfast, and he wasn't any hotter than he's been."

"No," Aunt Priscilla said, without turning around. "It happened sometime between then and an hour ago when I went over to feed him. I knew he'd been fretful, but I was busy and didn't pay that much attention."

It was obvious she was feeling bad.

"He often sounds fretful, Aunt Priscilla," Maggie said.

"Just what I told her," Mrs. Vanderpool agreed.

"What can we do?" Maggie said.

"I don't know. That's the awful part. I just don't know."

"I'm sorry," Maggie said, going up beside her and looking in the crib.

William's face was quite red. Putting a hand

to his cheek and head Maggie felt how hot he was. "His fever's gone up a lot."

"I know," Aunt Priscilla said, "but I don't know what to do about it, and the nearest doctor is in the town beyond ours."

Nine

For two days Maggie helped Aunt Priscilla and Mrs. Vanderpool try to break William's fever. They would bathe his face and neck in cool water and the fever would go down awhile. But then it would go back up. Maggie offered to stay home from school but was sent off firmly by Aunt Priscilla. "There's no reason for your staying here, Maggie. You're a great help, but I can certainly handle William alone for a few hours. And Mother is here."

"I'd go for Dr. Wright," Uncle James said once, "but Rumpkin is lame and I think it would permanently damage him and we'd have to shoot him."

So they bathed William again and were relieved to see the fever fall. But then it soared up again, higher than before.

Other than bathe his face and head there was nothing they could do. He refused to eat. His usually lively face was red and he cried fretfully.

Each time Maggie looked at him he seemed sicker. Her heart ached for Aunt Priscilla and Uncle James.

"Do you think William will die?" Annie whispered one night to Maggie when they were lying in bed.

"Oh Annie, I don't know. I pray not. But I've never seen a baby so sick."

Then one morning Uncle James said, "Whether Rumpkin's lame or not, I'm going to ride and get Sam Wright."

Much as she cared for William, Maggie felt a sharp thrust of worry. She loved Rumpkin. To ride him now would almost certainly damage him badly enough so that he'd have to be shot.

Uncle James was about to go to the barn when there was a knock on the door.

"Who on earth can that be?" Uncle James said. He opened the door. Maggie, just home from school, peered over his shoulder and was astonished to see Uncle Michael standing there.

"Uncle Michael!" she said.

Uncle Michael came into the cabin. "I've been to a lawyer, Mr. Russell, and made a deposition

125

about the fact that Maggie and Annie are my nieces and I have the right to take them back with me to New York. He said it would stand up in any court you want to take me to. So here is a copy." He laid a folded piece of paper on the table.

No one said anything. They all stood frozen. After a moment, Michael Casey asked, "What's going on?"

Maggie said, "William is terribly ill, Uncle Michael. His fever keeps going up."

Annie blurted out, "We're afraid he's going to die."

"He will die unless a doctor can be brought," Uncle James said. "We've done everything we know how, and it's obvious he's getting sicker."

"Isn't there a doctor in the community here?" Uncle Michael asked.

"No." Uncle James turned to his wife. "I'm going to have to take Rumpkin, even though he's lame. If he falls, he falls, but . . . but William's our son." He started for the door.

"Hold on there," Uncle Michael said. He strode over and looked in the crib. "Ach, the poor lad, he does indeed look sick. Where does the doctor live?"

"In Enright, about ten miles southwest of here."

He turned to James. "Your horse is lame?"

126

"Yes."

There was a pause. Then Michael said, "What's the doctor's name?"

"Dr. Wright. Samuel Wright."

"I'll find him and bring him back. You don't want to lose your horse, not even for this." Michael turned and went back out the door.

As he took hold of his horse's reins Aunt Priscilla, who had come to the door, said, "If you do this for us, there's no way we can show you our gratitude."

Uncle Michael stared at her a minute, started to say something, then stopped. Instead, he got on his horse and rode away at a canter and then a gallop. Maggie watched him go across the fields and out of sight.

She wondered if the Russells' gratitude would make them let Uncle Michael take her and Annie back to New York. Then she felt guilty for even thinking such a thing, or for worrying about herself at a time like this. She did not want to leave the Russells. The last of her anger at Uncle James died. She loved him as she did Aunt Priscilla. And she knew they loved her and that she and Annie belonged here with them.

The day wore on. She and Aunt Priscilla and Mrs. Vanderpool took turns bathing William's face in cool water and getting more water from the well.

"I worry so that he might get worse if we get him too cold," Aunt Priscilla said.

"And if we don't," Uncle James replied, "he could die from his fever. We've seen it happen to the children of other people out here."

When Annie came in after taking care of Bessie and the chickens, Maggie said to her, "What have you been doing, Annie?"

"Bringing Bessie in and milking her and feeding the rooster and the chickens."

"But I saw you sitting out there near the well. You never do that. Are you afraid of catching William's illness?"

"Of course not. I was praying to the Blessed Virgin. I begged her to make William better."

Maggie stared at Annie a minute, then hugged her sister. "I hope she listened to you," she said.

It was later in the day when two horsemen, riding rapidly, were sighted at some distance from the cabin. In a short time they were dismounting and tying their horses to a tree.

"Thank the Lord, you're here, Sam," Uncle James said, going out to meet them. "I don't know whether you can save William or not, but I didn't want him to go . . . to go . . . to go without your being here to do your best," James said.

Maggie saw then the tears in his eyes. "He's

our son, Sam, our only child." He stopped. "Our only child."

Maggie looked up, feeling the pain at his words.

Dr. Wright, carrying a bag, went to the crib, bending over it.

After a few minutes he straightened. "What have you been doing for him?"

"We didn't know what to do, Sam," Aunt Priscilla said, "except put cool cloths around his face and head."

"Get his clothes off," Dr. Wright ordered, "and fill a bowl full of your coldest water."

"Couldn't it kill him?" Uncle James said.

"Yes. It could. But this is pneumonia, and if we don't lower the fever somehow, his brain will be affected and it will almost certainly kill him. If we put him in cold water and denatured alcohol there's just a chance it might finally bring the fever down."

"Isn't there anything — any medicine — you can give him?"

"I've brought some that might help, but I'm not sure whether it will do any good."

Maggie held William as Dr. Wright, taking a spoon from Aunt Priscilla, filled it with a dark liquid from a bottle in his bag. Then, holding William's mouth open, he tipped in the contents of the spoon.

In the meantime Aunt Priscilla had filled a bowl from a bucket that her husband had just brought back from the well. The doctor emptied a bottle of clear liquid into the water. "Now," he said, "let's lower William into the bowl, and everybody say a prayer."

They held him in the water what seemed to Maggie a long time, though it was probably only a few seconds. William let out a cry. The doctor raised him, then, after another moment, lowered him into the chilled well water again.

William let out another, louder cry. After another few seconds the doctor raised him again and then lowered him a third time, and then a fourth.

"Now dry him and put him down," the doctor said. "If . . . if the fever goes up, put him in the bowl again. I'm afraid that's all I can do."

He sat for a while beside William's crib, checking his fever from time to time. Then he got up. "It's in God's hands now," he said.

The hours passed slowly. Aunt Priscilla sat beside William's crib, her hand on the side, rocking it slightly. William, his face now almost pale, lay still and soundless. Sometimes Mrs. Vanderpool sat with them, and once Maggie saw the older woman's hand rest on her daughter's as it lightly gripped the crib. Neither woman spoke.

Maggie busied herself as much as she could, washing, cleaning up, preparing dinner. Mrs. Vanderpool came over once to help her and then went back to her room. Watching her walk, Maggie knew she was feeling the pain in her back that she experienced when tired or tense or under a strain. Every now and then Maggie would look up at Aunt Priscilla, sitting so quietly, without moving or speaking, as though everything except her body were in another realm. Once she went up to her and said, "Aunt Priscilla, you haven't had anything to eat. You didn't even have breakfast. May I bring you something — some soup or bread?"

Aunt Priscilla replied without moving or looking at her. "No, thank you, Maggie. I'm not hungry."

There was something about the way she spoke — so different from her usual manner — that made Maggie feel rebuffed. As though she doesn't want to talk to me, she thought, and then, she's worried out of her mind, she told herself, and repeated it to Annie who came in and went over to see William. Maggie went up to the crib with her, and then pulled her back before she could say anything or ask any questions.

"I don't think Aunt Priscilla wants to talk right now."

"You mean she doesn't want to talk to us," Annie said.

"Not now, Annie." After a moment Maggie asked, "Did Uncle Michael leave?"

"No. He's in the barn with Uncle James putting cold wraps around Rumpkin's foot."

Maggie sighed. "Uncle Michael's been very good."

"Does that mean we have to go back to New York with him?"

"Oh Annie, I don't know . . . I don't know what we have to do." She was filled with despair. For the first time since their arrival in Kansas she felt like an interloper, someone who was not accepted, who didn't and never would really belong.

When Annie didn't reply, Maggie looked at her sister. "Do you? Want to go, I mean?"

"No. At least, I don't want to go now."

"What do you mean?"

"I don't know. Sometimes I remember things I liked."

"What kind of things?"

"Oh, like when we were outside that theater on Broadway, near Astor Place. All the dancing girls and actresses were going in before the first show. It was exciting! I loved it and sometimes I imagine me doing that. How wonderful it would be."

"But, Annie, when they weren't acting, those girls led harsh lives."

"Yes, I know. They were hungry sometimes."

"That's why Ma wanted us to come out here. I still don't know why you liked it — I mean the theater and the girls." Maggie heard the note of disapproval in her voice. But she knew it was also fear. Annie's so young, she thought. She doesn't know what it could be like. Out here she's safe.

She watched Annie tiptoe over to the crib, ready to pull her away if necessary. Annie whispered to Aunt Priscilla, "William looks better, doesn't he?"

Aunt Priscilla nodded, then said, "Yes, he does, Annie. I pray he stays looking better, then I'll know the fever's gone."

Annie went out again just as Uncle James came in. He went over to the crib and carried on a low-voiced conversation with his wife. Maggie couldn't hear what they said, but she imagined she was telling him the same things she'd said to Annie.

After a minute Uncle James looked into the crib. He reached down and touched his son's cheek. "He is cooler," he said. Then he turned and left the house.

It had been dark an hour when Aunt Priscilla said, "I'm almost afraid to say this, but William's face is still not red and he's still cool." She got up. "Maggie, would you come over here and watch him while I get supper?"

A few minutes later Annie said, "Where's Uncle Michael?"

"He's outside with James," Aunt Priscilla said. She glanced at them and then looked away.

Maggie sat and watched William. His face certainly looked a normal color. "Please let him be all right," she found herself silently praying.

A while later Aunt Priscilla said to Annie, "Run out to the barn, Annie, and tell Uncle James and your uncle Michael that supper is almost ready."

A few minutes later Uncle James came in. "Annie said William is better. Is it true?"

Aunt Priscilla smiled. "See for yourself."

Uncle James was already at the crib, standing beside Maggie, staring down at his son. Then he bent and touched his face. "He's still cool," he said wonderingly. He held his hand against William's face for a minute. "Maybe . . . maybe he's recovered," he said, his voice more unsure, more tentative, than Maggie could ever remember hearing it.

"God willing," Aunt Priscilla said. "And

134

thanks to Michael Casey." She looked up at her husband as she spoke.

"Yes," he said. He rubbed his eyes. "I've said that to him."

There was a silence. There was a question Maggie was sick to ask, but didn't dare.

Aunt Priscilla got up. "I'm going out to the barn to ask your uncle to join us at supper."

"I've already asked him," Uncle James said. "He said he'd stay out there keeping an eye on Rumpkin and putting compresses on his foot."

"But he has to eat something!"

"I told him that. But he said he'd be grateful if one of the girls could bring him out a plate and a cup of coffee."

"Are you sure?"

"Priscilla, I've asked him as warmly and as sincerely as I know how to join us. But I don't think he wants to."

"I see. Then I'll prepare a plate for him."

But when Maggie and Annie went out carrying a plate of food, a knife and fork, a napkin and a cup of coffee, they found their uncle sound asleep in a pile of hay not far from Rumpkin.

"Should I wake him up, Maggie?" Annie whispered.

Maggie was at Rumpkin's side, stroking his nose and letting him nuzzle her hand. "Yes. I guess so. He ought to eat while it's hot."

Annie bent over her uncle's form. "Uncle Michael," she said in her clear, carrying voice. "We have your supper here."

He opened his eyes and stared at her a moment. Then he made a sound and sat up. "Annie, me girl," he said, and rubbed his face.

"How is Rumpkin, Uncle Michael?" Maggie asked.

"He'll be fine, if he doesn't use that foot for a day or two more." He rubbed his face again. "How is William?"

"It looks like he's going to be fine, too. Thanks to you."

He grunted and started to get to his feet.

"Don't you want your supper while you're sitting down? Here!" Maggie took over the plate and utensils and put them on the mound of hay beside him. Annie handed him the coffee.

He looked up and smiled. "Come now, sit here beside me." And he patted the pile of hay near him.

Annie promptly sat down. "Come on, Mag."

"We ought . . ." Maggie started, then sat down beside Annie.

Uncle Michael smiled, reminding Maggie suddenly of her mother before she became ill, when she was still a lovely young woman.

"What is it, Maggie?" he asked gently.

Maggie put her hands up and felt the tears.

136

"You make me think of Ma," she said. He reached across and touched her cheek. "She'd be proud of you, Maggie, of you both."

There was a short silence. Annie had found Blackie and was playing with him.

Finally unable to contain her anxiety any longer, tortured by her inner feeling of being divided, Maggie burst out, "Uncle Michael, are you going to —"

"Ah, Maggie," he interrupted her, looking up. He reached his long arm up and grasped her hand. She felt as though her divided heart would break. At least with him, back in New York, she would feel accepted, not always judged. But here in Kansas — images of Aunt Priscilla, Mrs. Vanderpool, Uncle James, and finally Tom went through her mind, bringing pain. Her eyes strayed outside to the rolling fields which she had come to love.

"Don't be asking me a lot of questions now, Maggie," Uncle Michael said, squeezing her hand.

His voice was filled with sadness, too, Maggie thought.

He said gently, "Now leave me have me supper in peace!"

Ten

Two mornings later Maggie woke up early. It was the day of the school picnic. Her body felt stiff and she realized she'd been lying rigid, something she'd done since childhood when she was worried. Trying not to wake Annie, who was sprawled, sound asleep, at her side, she turned over and saw the sunlight pouring into the window. Her spirits, low anyway, sank further.

If only it had rained, they would have been forced to abandon, or at least postpone, the picnic! But it was a fine spring morning. Lying there, her face on the pillow, staring out the window, she found herself dreading the day, something she hadn't done more than two or three times since she'd been out here in Kansas with the Russells, and the other times went back to the days when she knew she couldn't read and was afraid of being shown up in class.

Thinking of that made her think again of Tom, whom she had been trying desperately to keep out of her mind. But she could no longer push him out. It was almost as though he were there beside her. Quietly, Maggie cried, something she seldom allowed herself to do. No, she thought, she still didn't know how she felt about going back to New York, but she wished that she were anywhere else today rather than going to the picnic.

The fact that her sixteenth birthday would take place this month added to her misery. The Russells had always celebrated their birthdays with cake and festivities. And sixteen was an unofficial step into being a young woman. Girls they all knew and had been to school with had married when they were sixteen. I suppose Ellen is sixteen, too, Maggie thought miserably. It was too much. The tears started again, but this time she resisted them and sat up.

"What time is it?" Annie asked, yawning.

"Time for breakfast," Maggie said.

"I wonder how William is," Annie said.

Maggie felt guilty that among her other early morning thoughts was not one concerning William.

Quickly she threw back the covers and pulled on her clothes, relieved to see that William's crib was still in the Russells' bedroom. She felt sure that if something were wrong they'd all be out in the main room.

Then she saw the cabin door open and Aunt Priscilla come in from the outside carrying some milk. "How's William?" Maggie asked.

Aunt Priscilla smiled. "I'm delighted to say he seems fine — his temperature normal. He even sounds hungry!"

"I'm so glad! Look, Aunt Priscilla, why don't you let me stay with him while the rest of you go to the picnic?"

She didn't really think Aunt Priscilla would be deceived as to her motive, and she was right.

"No, Maggie, I'm not going. William's been so sick. And if I were there, I'd just be worrying myself to death. But James and Mother will be going." She paused. "I know you don't want to go, but I don't think not going will accomplish anything except letting the whole class know how you feel."

"Is that so bad?" Maggie asked rather bitterly.

"You don't think so now, but you will, later."

Maggie knew she was right, but it didn't make things any easier. "All right."

Aunt Priscilla glanced at Maggie. "When I was out in the barn getting milk I asked Mr.

Casey if he wanted to go on the picnic with you."

Maggie glanced at her in surprise. "Is he going to?"

"He didn't really give an answer. But I think he might. He . . . he feels very family-like with you and Annie."

"But how're we going to get there? Rumpkin isn't well enough yet, is he, to pull the wagon?"

"No, although he seems a lot better. But James borrowed your uncle's horse to go over and ask the Schmidts if we could go in their wagon with them. It's a bigger wagon than ours."

"That's nice. I like Rachel," Maggie said.

"Yes. I know you do."

"Is Uncle James back?"

"Not yet."

But when Uncle James came back he said he'd seen the Schmidts' wagon and he didn't think it was big enough for all the Schmidts and four of them.

Maggie's spirits rose. "I'll stay home with you and William," she said.

"No, Maggie," Aunt Priscilla said firmly. "James, perhaps Mr. Casey might change his mind about going to the picnic and you could use his horse."

"I'll ask him," Uncle James said, and went into the barn.

A few minutes later Maggie saw the two men come out. "Well," Uncle Michael said, grinning a little, "it seems like I'll be going on your picnic with you after all."

Aunt Priscilla, Maggie, and Annie spent the next hour making sandwiches and putting them and a pie Aunt Priscilla had made earlier into a basket. There was a stream near the lake with freshwater, so they also packed cups for that and they brought in a container for the milk.

At the last moment Mrs. Vanderpool grumbled, "I don't much like picnics." She ignored a glance from her daughter. "I think I'll stay home, too, and keep Priscilla and William company."

"Mama!" Aunt Priscilla protested.

"No, Priscilla, I really don't want to go."

Her daughter sighed. "Very well." She glanced at Maggie. "I'm sorry, my dear. But you'll have James and your uncle Michael and, of course, Annie. And try to have a good time! It's beautiful around the lake, but be careful! I'm told it's quite deep at one end."

"Yes, Aunt Priscilla." Maggie hoped she didn't sound as low as she felt.

The Russells were among those farthest away from the picnic site, so they were among the last to arrive. Uncle James and Uncle Michael unhitched the horse and set him to graze in the nearby field among the other horses from the wagons. Then everyone helped in unpacking the wagon, spreading the big tablecloth they'd brought along, and talking to the Schmidts and the Carters, who had settled themselves nearby.

There was a little speech by Miss Bailey, saying the picnic was in honor of the graduating class. She congratulated the boys and girls who would soon finish school and asked them to stand up and be applauded.

Then Brother Evans said grace. Maggie glanced anxiously at Uncle Michael when the minister told everyone to bow his head, but Uncle Michael lowered his along with the others.

Maggie, her heart thumping painfully, had, from the time they'd arrived, busied herself with the unpacking and kept her gaze on what she was doing and what was immediately in front of her. But after Miss Bailey's speech and Brother Evans's grace, with little more to do, it was impossible not to look around.

All the class was there with their families, their picnic cloths spread out under the trees around the lake and sometimes almost touching. There was plenty of food: meat pies, cooked chicken legs and breasts, bread, cake,

fruit pies, coffee, and milk. Maggie found herself remembering the hungry days in New
York. Where would Annie and I be, she
thought, if we hadn't been sent here? A wave
of gratitude washed over her. Kansas had become her home. She looked over at the trees
and the clear lake water and the rolling land
beyond. How dear this was. She'd felt it before,
but not quite like this.

Uncle Michael doesn't understand, she
thought. Was there any way she could make
him understand? She looked at him, wondering how to start. But his attention was else-
where — he was watching Miss Bailey, who
was sitting with some of the substitute teachers. Maggie saw Mrs. Gresham and noted Mrs.
Smiley's sour face.

Not far from the teachers was the Mc-
Candless tribe, with Ellen's golden head turning this way and that as she greeted various
— usually male — classmates. Ellen's sister,
Hannah, was sitting as far away from Ellen as
she could. It was when it became obvious that
Ellen's attention kept coming back and con-
centrating in one particular direction beyond
the Russells' picnic cloth that Maggie couldn't
stop herself from turning and looking.

The Brintons, father and son, were under a
tree a little distance from the lake. Since there
were only the two of them, their cloth was two

144

napkins put together, and they seemed to be keeping to themselves, neither looking up. Her heart gave a thump. At that moment Ellen caught Maggie looking at the Brintons, and gave a knowing grin.

Maggie felt her face grow hot and she looked away quickly. Taking a silent vow not to be caught again, she determined to keep her face turned in the opposite direction. But, while passing things and answering friendly comments from other groups around, she inevitably caught sight of Tom and his father and, one time, she was surprised to see Tom looking fixedly at her.

"That's the young feller who asked the question about Parliament, isn't it, Maggie?"

Maggie, caught between wanting to disclaim any knowledge of him and knowing she couldn't, started, "Er —"

"That's Tom Brinton, Uncle Michael," Annie said. "I told you he's kind of sweet on Maggie."

"He is not," Maggie said angrily before she could stop herself.

"Well, he was before . . ." Annie, suddenly remembering the fight and who was involved, glanced at Uncle James and faltered to a stop.

Uncle Michael frowned. "Before what, Annie?"

"Before Paul Brinton, young Tom's father, and I had a fight," Uncle James said calmly.

"Oh," Uncle Michael said and then broke into a laugh. "There now, I thought it was only the Irish that had that kind of trouble."

"There's Jenny Barton," Annie said, waving at one of her classmates down near the lake.

Jenny waved back. She and her parents and two sisters were having their picnic on a rock above the water.

"Uncle James, I think I'll go and see Jenny," Annie said.

"All right." He glanced at Michael Casey as Annie ran off. It was obvious to Maggie that the tension between the two men had not relaxed or lessened. When she thought of the trouble that would certainly ensue if Uncle Michael went through with the lawsuit, she wondered if it would be easier for the Russells if she and Annie just agreed to go with him. And perhaps, she thought, having William now, Uncle James might not care so much if they did go. She glanced at him and then away, torn by conflicting feelings.

And Aunt Priscilla — but she couldn't bear to think of not having Aunt Priscilla in her life.

How horribly complicated it all was. . . . And how would the Russells feel, after all the care and affection they'd lavished on her and Annie?

It would be easier, she found herself thinking strangely, if Uncle Michael and Uncle James were all-out enemies: They could fight without regret. But Uncle Michael had gone to get the doctor for William when he almost certainly would have died. It was very confusing and muddling.

She glanced down toward the Bartons and saw Annie and Jenny chasing each other and laughing and shrieking, running over the rocks that edged the lake. "If those two don't watch out they'll fall in," Uncle Michael said.

It was at that moment Maggie heard Mrs. Smiley's unmistakable voice. "Yes, I know people say he's nice, but I still think it's pretty strange having a Roman from New York in this part of the country. That's what you get when you take in children you know nothing about. Not what we want or are used to."

Maggie felt her whole body go tense. She saw the two men stiffen. Uncle James started to get up. Uncle Michael was already on his feet.

At that moment there was a scream. Maggie jumped up. Uncle James said, "Annie's fallen in," and started running.

There were shouts and yells. Everything was a blur, but she could hear her own voice crying, "Annie, Annie."

"Can she swim?" one of the neighbors asked as he ran down the slope toward the water.

Of course not, Maggie thought. Running, she could see Annie's head and arms above the water, waving. Then they disappeared.

Maggie was near the water, running with all the other neighbors when she saw a figure dive off the rock and realized it was Tom. He came up with Annie in the bend of one arm and started moving with the other toward the shore.

"Well done, Tom!" It was Miss Bailey's voice and there were other cries of "Well done," "Good lad!" and so on. Maggie had reached the shore just as Miss Bailey, holding a cloth, wrapped Annie up as Tom pushed her and Miss Bailey lifted her out of the water.

"Are you all right, Annie?" Miss Bailey asked.

"Yes, I'm fine," Annie said, and apart from being soaking wet, she looked it.

"I think I'd better dry you off," Miss Bailey said, and then, "Mrs. Russell isn't here today, is she?"

"No," Maggie said, helping the teacher soak up some of the wet of Annie's clothes. "She stayed to make sure William was all right."

"Why don't we take her behind those trees over there and dry her off properly?" Miss Bailey said. "And if anyone has an extra blouse or skirt, we can give her dry clothes long enough to get her back."

All sorts of garments were produced and Maggie and Miss Bailey took Annie behind the little cluster of trees and stripped her wet clothes off.

"Maggie, go out and see if your uncle can get the wagon hitched up to take Annie and you back. It's going to get cooler around here once the sun goes down."

"Yes, all right," Maggie said.

When she got nearer to their picnic place she saw the cloth folded up and both men standing beside the wagon with Uncle Michael's horse hitched up.

"Ready to take her back?" Uncle James asked.

"Yes."

"All right. But there's something I have to do first. Bring her here in the meantime."

As Maggie and Miss Bailey brought the partially clothed, partially wrapped Annie from behind the trees, Maggie saw Uncle James approach Tom. She saw him hold out his hand. They were near enough for her to hear him.

"That was a magnificent thing you did, Tom. We owe you a lot of thanks."

Tom blushed. Maggie saw him glance toward her. Shyly, he smiled. She hadn't forgotten anything, and she knew the hurt in her was still there. But she also saw that some things

149

were more important than others: Tom's sav-
ing Annie was one; so also was the fact that
she knew now, without doubt, that Tom liked
her, maybe felt about her the way she knew
now she felt about him. Where that certainty
came from she wasn't sure. But it was there,
and she smiled back.

Paul Brinton approached them. "Let's forget
about that stupid mess, James. The damn
war's over. I'm sorry for what I said."

"I am, too," Uncle James said. He smiled.
"And you must be very proud of Tom."

"Thanks. I am."

The two men shook hands, then looked a
little embarrassed and cleared their throats.

Annie, dressed in a borrowed sweater,
blouse, and skirt, and wrapped inside the two
men's jackets, seemed cheerful all the way
home. When they got there and Aunt Priscilla
was told what had happened, she put water
on to boil and hauled out the tin bath that was
used by everyone.

"You're going to get a good soaking in this
tonight, Annie."

"I'm not a bit cold, Aunt Priscilla."

"I know you're not. But I'm not taking any
risk. I'm going to pull this into our bedroom
and let you sit in it there until I'm convinced
any possible chill is gone."

A mixture of hot and cold water was poured

into the tub until Aunt Priscilla was sure it was the right temperature. Annie lowered herself into the tub and Maggie sat in the Russells' bedroom with her to keep her company.

Later Annie, sleepy from all that had happened to her, went to bed and straight to sleep. Beside her Maggie lay awake for a while, thinking about what had happened. The last thing she remembered before drifting off was the smile on Tom's face and there, in the dark, she smiled back.

The next morning before breakfast Uncle James came in from the barn. "Well, Rumpkin seems a lot better. Another day and he'll be fine, and I have plenty of work to do around here today."

"Is Mr. Casey coming in for breakfast?" Aunt Priscilla asked, her hand on the pan in which she was cooking eggs, bacon, and hoecakes.

At that moment he appeared in the doorway. He looked at his nieces, helping to lay the table, and they looked back.

Maggie felt the fear clutch at her again. "Uncle Michael —" she started, and then stopped, not sure how to go on without bringing about what she most feared.

Uncle Michael walked over to the table and stared back at her. "No, Maggie, no need to be looking at me like that." He took a breath and looked down at his hands, now gripping the back of a chair. "Last night I dreamed of your ma. We were children again, back in Ireland. She was always a great one for taking care of us younger ones. Somehow . . . somehow I knew she wanted you here. I understood, perhaps for the first time, why she'd sent you out, despite . . . well, despite her religion and the family and the rest. She wanted you and Annie to be safe." He paused again. "I've spent these past days trying to think clearly, as I was trained to. But there are times when . . . when thinking doesn't seem to do much good. It's just a muddle!"

There was a silence. Then he raised his head. "I'll not be seeing the lawyer again."

"If you really feel that . . ." Aunt Priscilla started, then stopped.

Uncle James cleared his throat. "I am truly glad. More . . . More than I — more than we can say! Maggie and Annie are dear to us."

Maggie looked at him and was astonished to see tears in his eyes.

"Uncle James," she said, "you really do . . . do want us to stay, don't you."

"Of course he does, Maggie dear," Aunt Priscilla said gently. "We all do."

"I know I've given you reason to wonder about it," Uncle James said. "And I'm sorry about that, very sorry. I don't know how to say this . . ." His voice trailed off.

Suddenly, impulsively, Maggie went over and hugged him and kissed his cheek. "It's all right, Uncle James. I know now you do."

"Oh, Uncle Michael," Annie cried. "When I'm grown up, I'll come see you again in New York."

"Will you now, Annie! Well, we'll write, won't we, Maggie?"

"Oh, yes, Uncle Michael. And you can come visit here again!" She turned toward the Russells. "Can't he, Uncle James, Aunt Priscilla?"

"Absolutely. You will always be most welcome." Uncle James and Aunt Priscilla spoke almost together.

"Ay, perhaps . . . perhaps I will. It's a grand place with grand people."

As clearly as though she could see in his mind, Maggie knew he was thinking about Miss Bailey. But neither mentioned her name.

Annie did, though. "I bet Miss Bailey might be pleased to see you, Uncle Michael!"

"Listen to you," he said. But he smiled.

"Oh, Uncle Michael!" For the first time Maggie went over and embraced him. "I'm glad you came."

He put his arm around her. "Are you now, Maggie? There've been times when I thought you weren't at all happy about it."

"I . . . I wasn't, when I thought you would make us leave here."

"Well, I'll not be doing that. There are good people in New York, too, Maggie. But you're right. Everything is much harder, specially for two girls. May God and the Church forgive me, but you're better off here. I know that now, for sure."

He straightened. "I'll be taking my leave now."

"Uncle Michael," Maggie and Annie cried. They ran toward him.

He put his arms around them and hugged them close. "Ach now, ye'll be making me disgrace meself. When I get settled I'll write." He paused. "And . . . And Maggie, tell Miss Bailey that I'll be writing, will ye?"

"Yes. Of course I will." Impulsively she added, "You like her, don't you, Uncle Michael? I saw your face when you were talking to her."

"Ay, I do, Maggie. It's a grand woman she is."

Maggie felt the tears come as she struggled with a mixture of feelings. She walked up to him. "Maybe . . . maybe, like Annie said, maybe you can come back."

"Maybe . . . it's a thought, Maggie." He leaned down and kissed her cheek. "And give my best wishes to young Brinton. He's a good lad."

When he saw Maggie's cheek go pink he

laughed and touched it. Then he looked down at his younger niece who had run up. "And don't, either of you, forget your people or where you come from."

"I still pray to the Blessed Virgin, Uncle Michael," Annie said.

"Do you now? I'm delighted to hear it, Annie."

"Ma's there with her, you know."

"Yes, she is, and praying for us all, and the Lord knows we need it." He leaned down and hugged and kissed her.

He shook hands with the Russells and Mrs. Vanderpool. Then he walked out of the cabin. They followed him outside. His horse was tethered to a nearby post. He mounted, turned, and waved. Then he rode away across the rolling prairie.

About the Author

ISABELLE HOLLAND is the author of more than fifty books for children and adults, including *The Journey Home* and *Behind the Lines*.

When asked why she wanted to continue the story of Maggie and Annie Lavin, Ms. Holland said, "I didn't want to say good-bye to them. I had to know what happened after *The Journey Home*, and the only way I could know or find out was by writing about them."

The daughter of a foreign service officer, Isabelle Holland was born in Basel, Switzerland, and grew up around the world, spending many years in Guatemala and England.

Ms. Holland now shares her home in New York City with four engaging cats.